DIVINE DICKS AND MORTAL PRICKS

Also by Walburga Appleseed

The Princess and the Prick

DIVINE DICKS AND MORTAL PRICKS

Greek Myths for Feminists

Walburga Appleseed

Illustrated by
Dàlia Adillon

ONE PLACE. MANY STORIES

HQ
An imprint of HarperCollins*Publishers* Ltd
1 London Bridge Street
London SE1 9GF

www.harpercollins.co.uk

HarperCollins*Publishers*
Macken House, 39/40 Mayor Street Upper,
Dublin 1, D01 C9W8, Ireland

This edition 2024

1
First published in Great Britain by
HQ, an imprint of HarperCollins*Publishers* Ltd 2024

Copyright © Anita Lehmann 2024

Designed by Siaron Hughes
Illustrated by Dàlia Adillon

Anita Lehmann asserts the moral right to be
identified as the author of this work.

A catalogue record for this book is
available from the British Library.

ISBN 978-0-00-866405-3

MIX
Paper | Supporting
responsible forestry
FSC™ C007454

This book contains FSC™ certified paper and other controlled
sources to ensure responsible forest management.

For more information visit: www.harpercollins.co.uk/green

Printed and Bound in the UK using 100% Renewable Electricity at
CPI Group (UK) Ltd, Croydon, CR0 4YY

To Harriet the poetess,
with thanks for her words.

Because of her, Odysseus will
always be a #MAMIL to me.

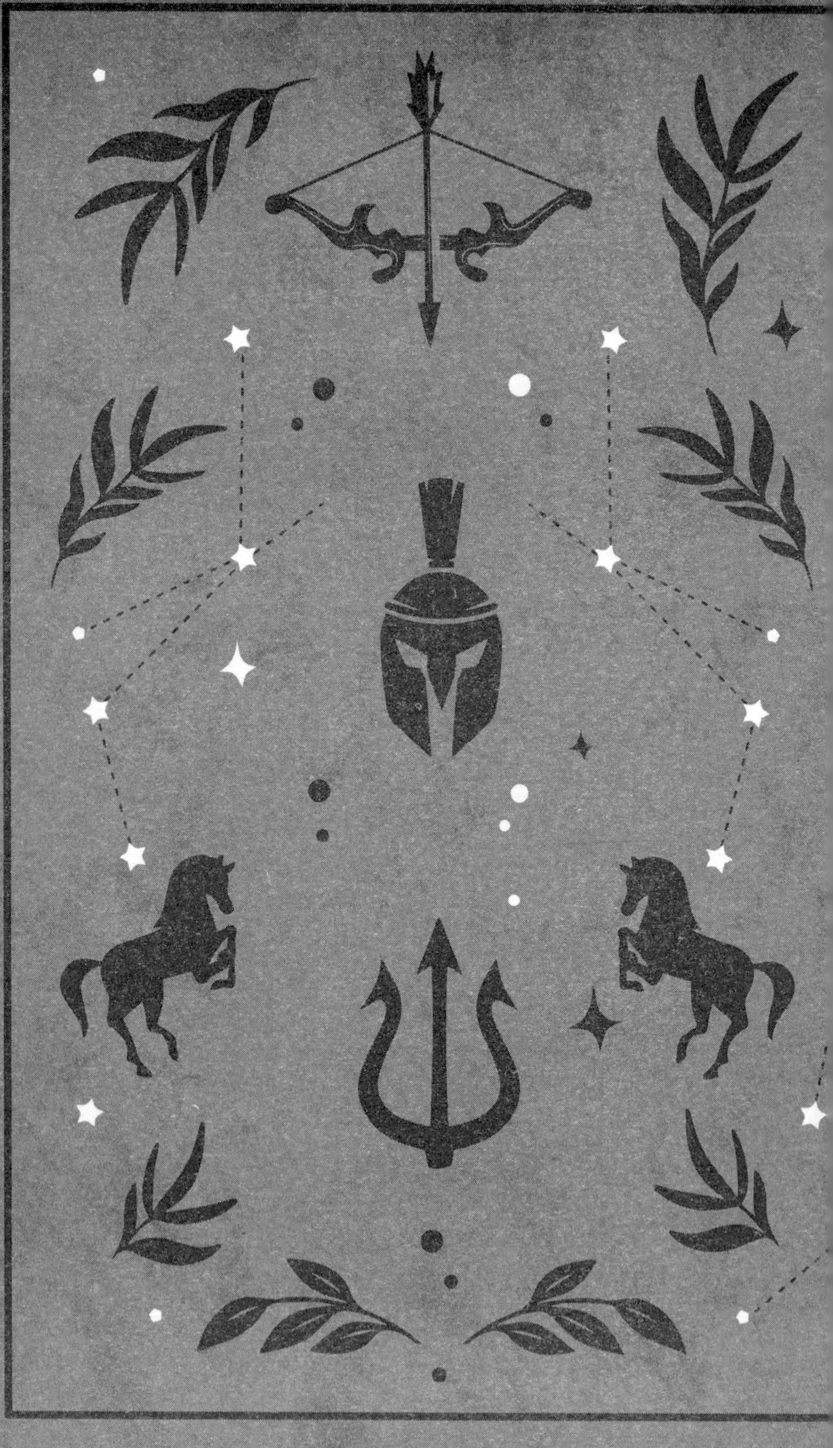

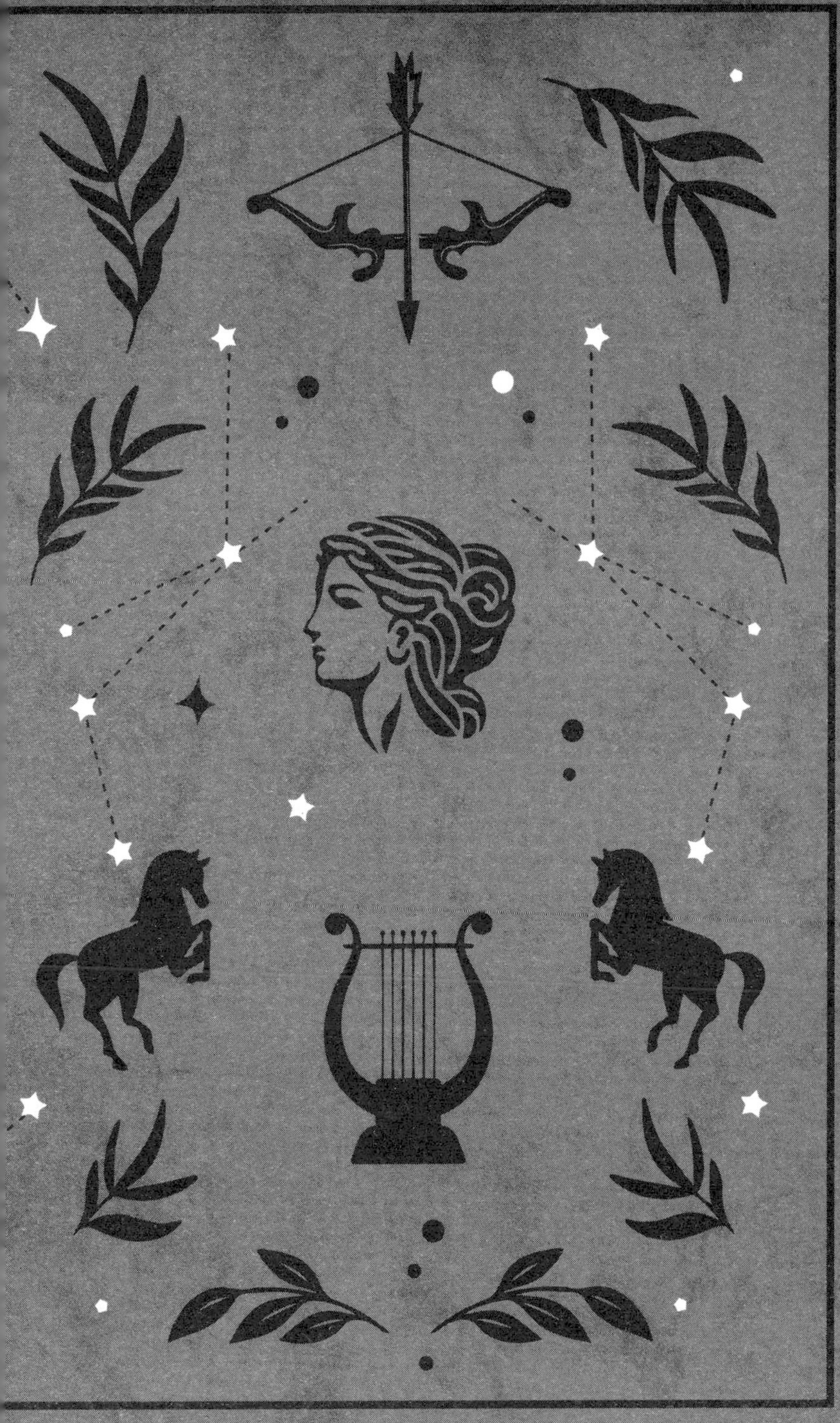

INTRODUCTION

In this book, you will find neither treatises about the complex nature of the Greek gods nor an analysis of, say, the role of the mighty spear in the *Iliad*. It won't be a deep dive into Zeus' psyche, either. Just his pants.

The Greek myths are such mad, fascinating stories that I can't help but love them. I also admire their longevity. After all, they have kept Europe entertained over many millennia. But every time I read them, they get up my nose. Seriously, Homer? What is it with all the gratuitous willy-waving? Why do the women get such a terrible deal? How do they deserve such absurd men? And what can I do about it?

My answer is this book.

Sexism is ridiculous. Let's laugh at it! Whether you're a complete newbie to Zeus' little fantasies or already have a PhD in Greek mythogyny, I hope that you too will be cackling at the sandal-clad patriarchy in no time.

With love,
Walburga Appleseed

FAMILY TREE:
THE OLYMPIAN GODS

CRONOS + RHEA

Dysfunctional titanic parents.
Just so happen to be siblings.

**APHRODITE,
GODDESS OF LOVE**

Born out of the waves and
her grandfather's testicles.
Shallow, pretty, and petty.

———————— Children of

— — — — Zeus' infidelity (two of many)

+ Marriage

LETO + ZEUS,
HEAD GOD ———————

APOLLO,
GOD OF ALL
SORTS

Complicated.
Fond of music.
Rapist.

ARTEMIS,
GODDESS OF
HUNTING

Stays the hell
away from
the men in her
family.

POSEIDON, GOD
OF THE SEA

A little bit fishy.

DEMETER,
GODDESS OF
AGRICULTURE

Fertile.

ZEUS,
HEAD GOD

Extremely fertile.
Part-time furry.
Serial rapist.

ATHENA,
GODDESS
OF WISDOM

Shallow, touchy,
and petty.

ARES,
GOD OF WAR

Handsome,
but brutal.

HERA, QUEEN
OF THE GODS,
SISTER AND
WIFE OF ZEUS

Shallow, jealous,
and petty.

HEPHAESTUS, THE
BLACKSMITH GOD

The only competent one.

HADES,
GOD OF THE
UNDERWORLD

On the dark side.

HESTIA,
GODDESS OF
THE HEARTH

Strong trad-wife
vibes.

Who's Who – Greek Myths

Epic Egos and Half-Baked Heroes

TLDR:
Greek Mythogyny

The Greek myths are mainly about men or gods (or both) raping women, trying to rape women, or failing to rape women.

Epic Egos and Half-Baked Heroes

PAN:

Goat-legged god. Fond of music.
Very furry.

EROS:

God of love. The controlling type.

JASON:

Adulterer. Hero.

HERACLES:

Perpetrator of domestic violence. Hero.

THESEUS:

Rapist. Hero.

PERSEUS:

Mediocre man bestowed gifts by the gods
for no obvious reason. Hero.

PENTHEUS:

Perv. Otherwise, quite nice.

NARCISSUS:

Selfish bastard.

ORPHEUS:

The sensitive, musical type.

OEDIPUS:

Complex.

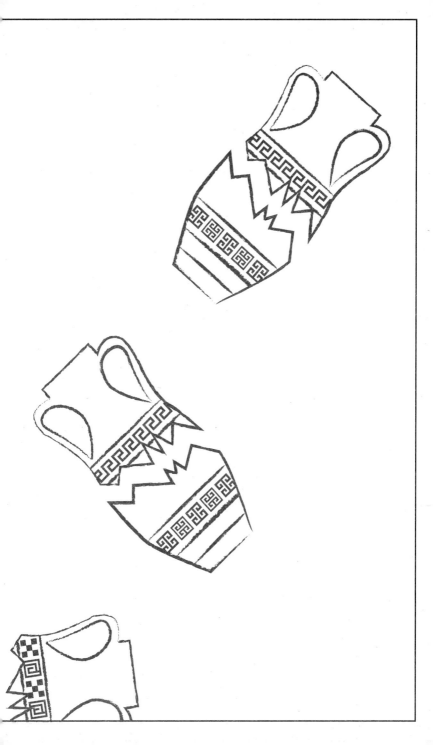

The Perfectly
Normal Women

ARIADNE:

Clever woman.

MEDUSA:

Angry woman.

ANDROMEDA:

Young woman.

EUROPA:

Pretty woman.

EURYDICE:

A pretty ordinary woman.

MEDEA:

Smart, angry woman.

THE AMAZONS:

Warrior women.

PSYCHE:

Fond of invisible men
with attachment issues.

ECHO:

A bit repetitive.

IO:

A bit of a cow.

PERSEPHONE:

Bored to death.

ARIADNE'S THREAD

'Ariadne's thread was a genius idea,'
said Theseus.

So, on reflection, it had probably been his.

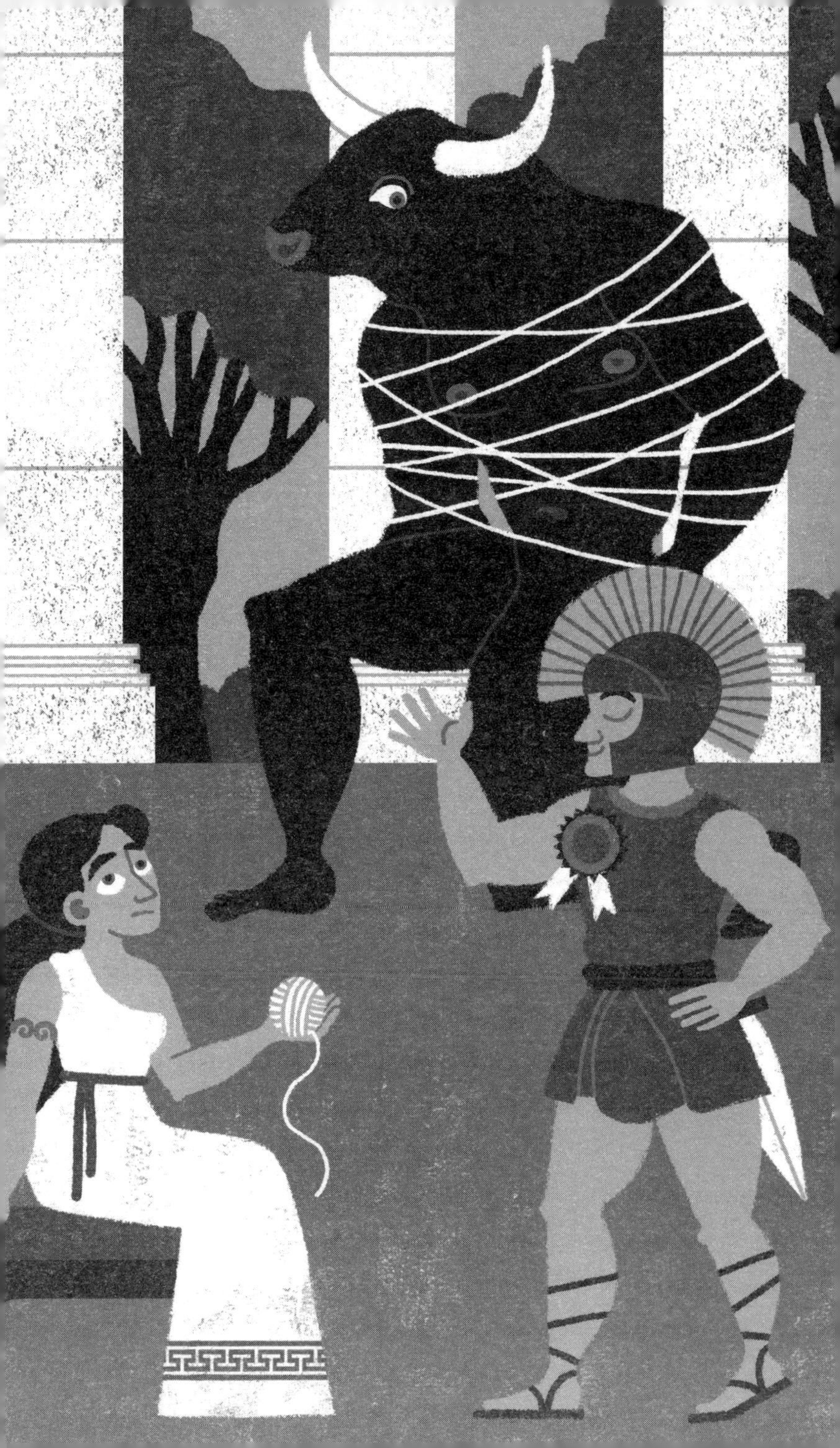

HADES AND PERSEPHONE

'I didn't want to come. You kidnapped me,' said Persephone, 'and you forced me to stay.'

'You never said "no",' said Hades.

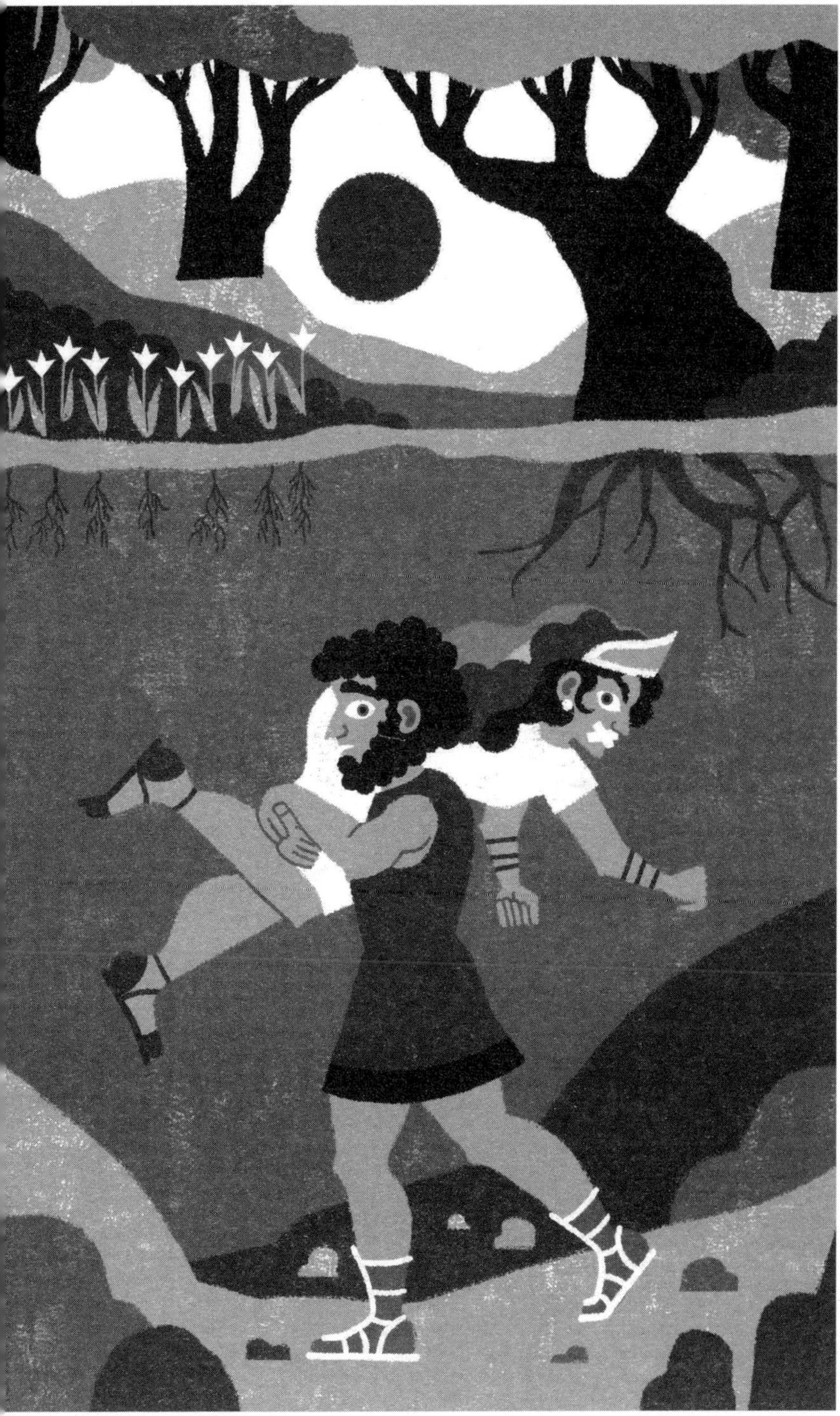

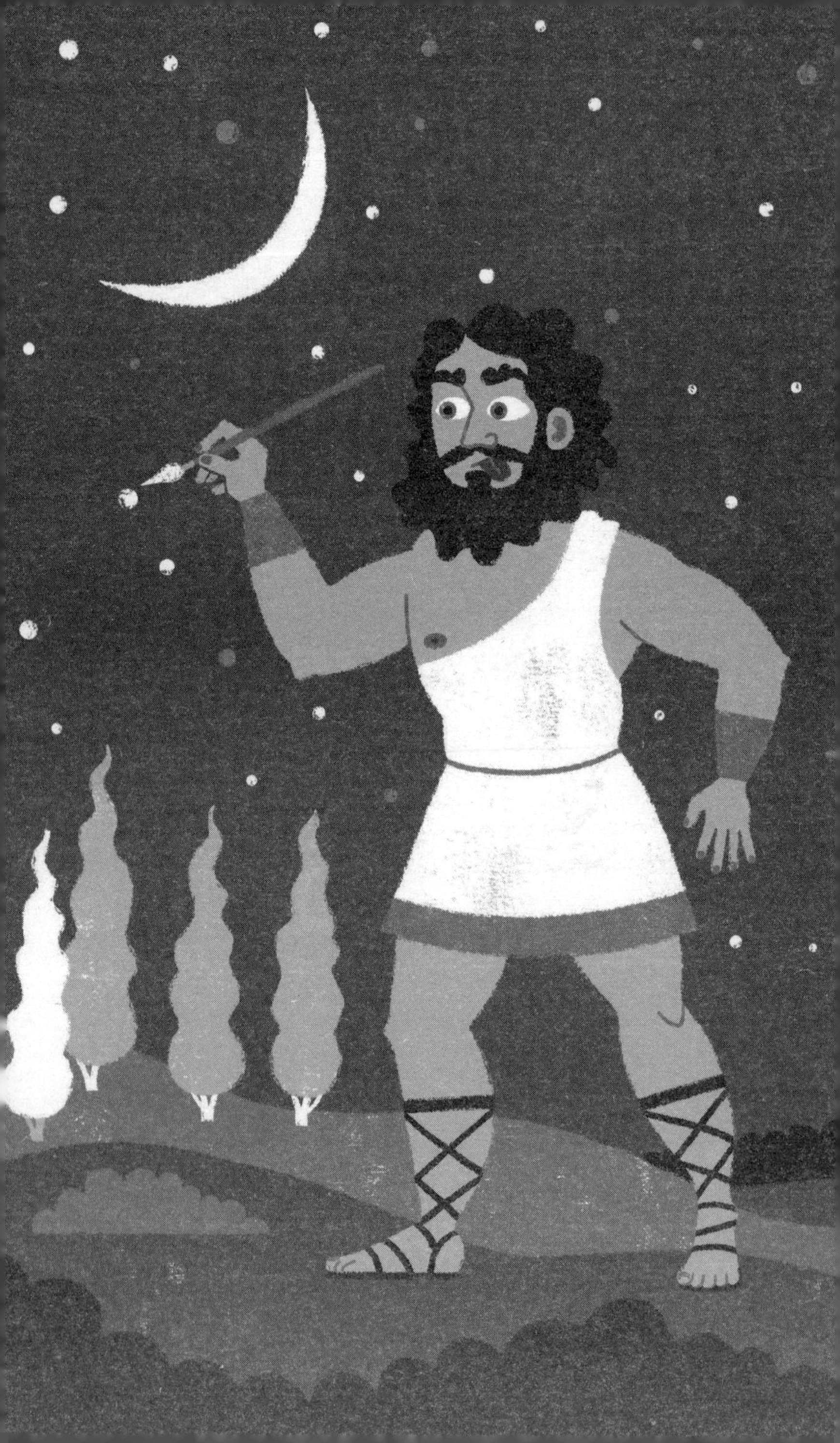

EUROPA AND ZEUS

Zeus seduced, abducted, and raped Europa.
Europa was sad.
Zeus said he'd name a star after her.
Still, Europa was sad.
Ungrateful woman.

MEDUSA

Ladies, beware: angry women grow
snakes in their hair.

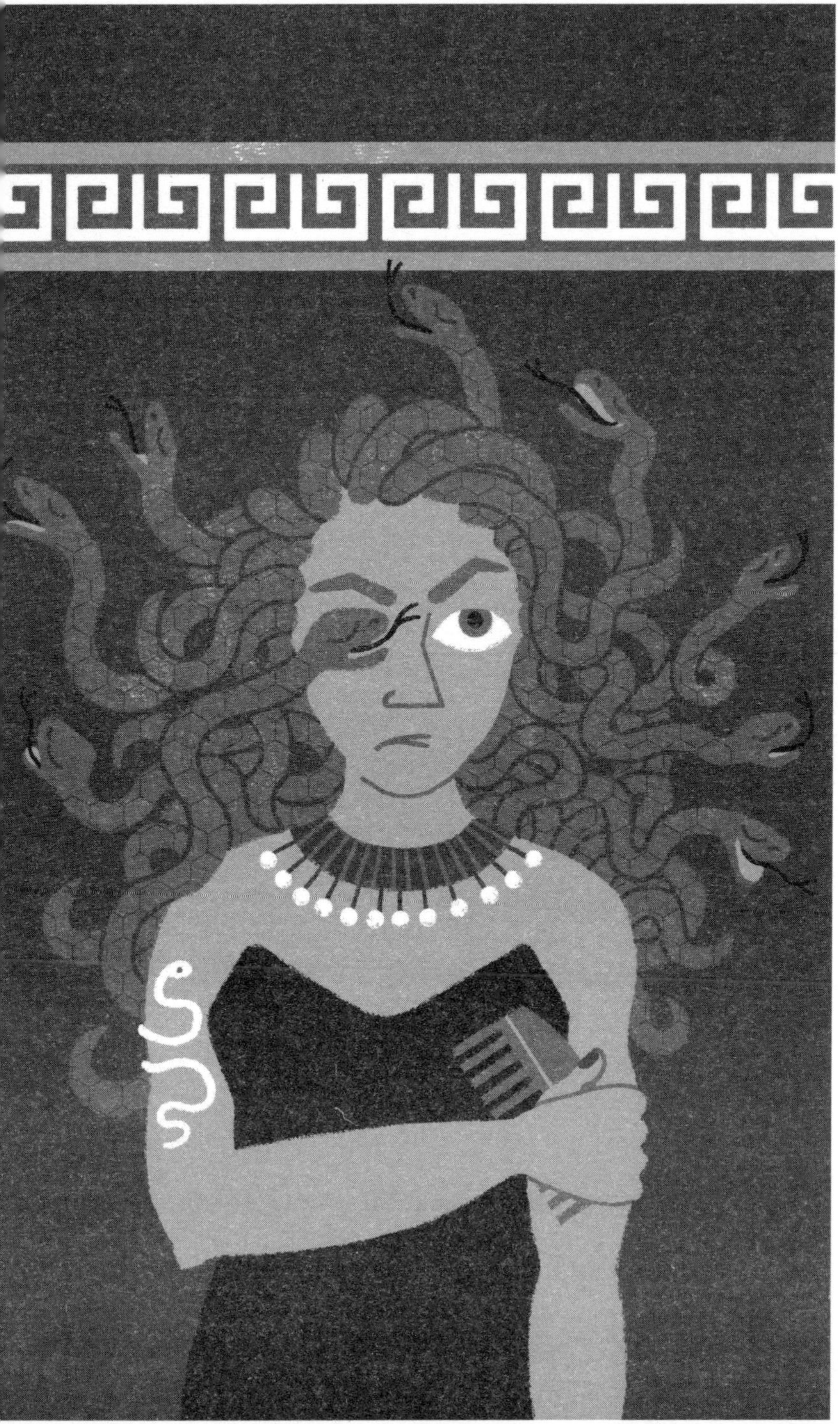

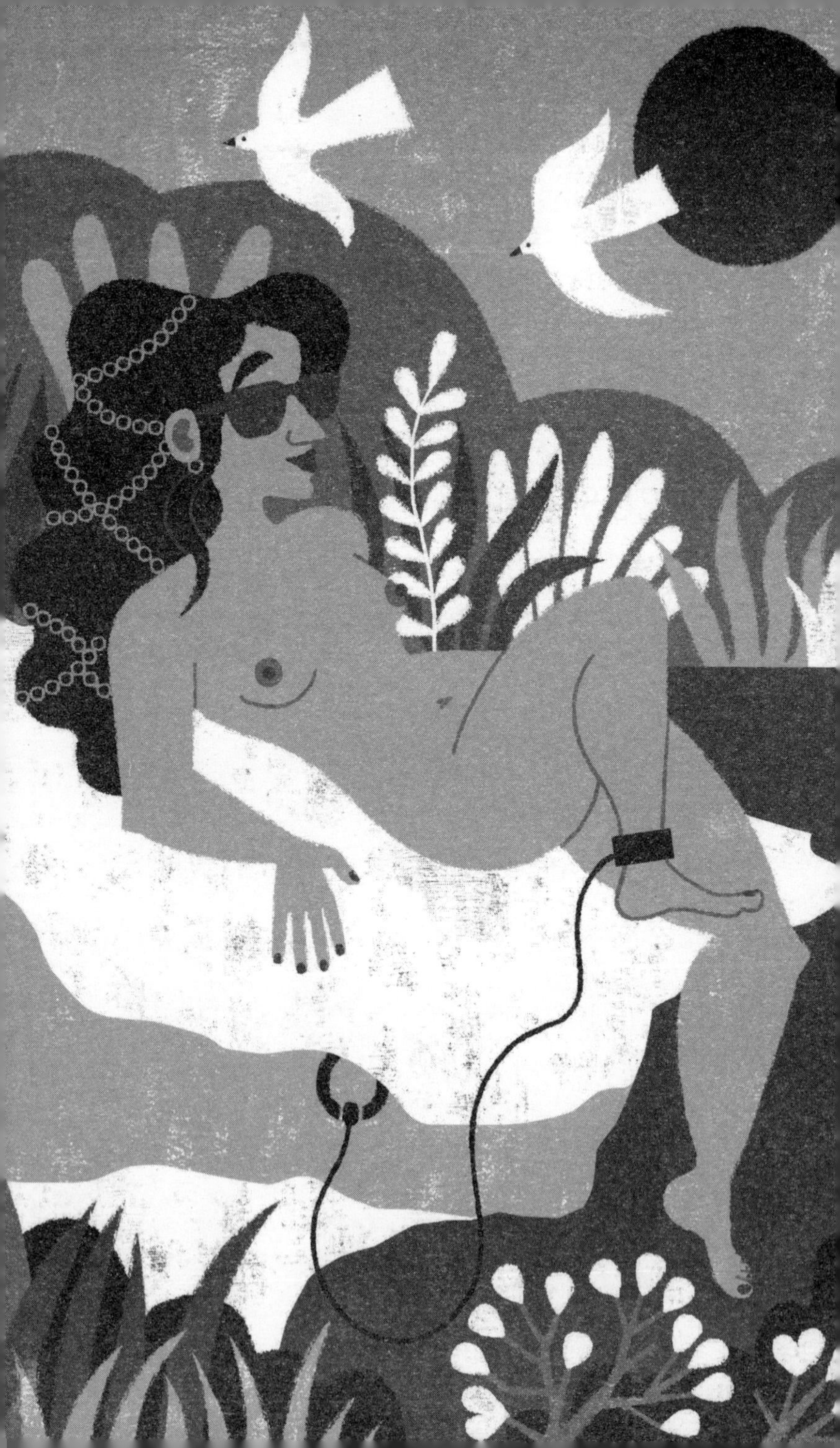

PERSEUS AND ANDROMEDA

A naked woman chained to a rock.

What's not to like?

ORPHEUS AND EURYDICE

'There is one thing you must remember,'
Eurydice said.
'Whatever you say, chickpea,' replied Orpheus.
'One important thing: you must not turn around,'
she said. 'Should I write it down for you?'
'No worries, I got it,' Orpheus said.
Halfway up from hell, he had forgotten what
she had said, so, he turned around to ask her.

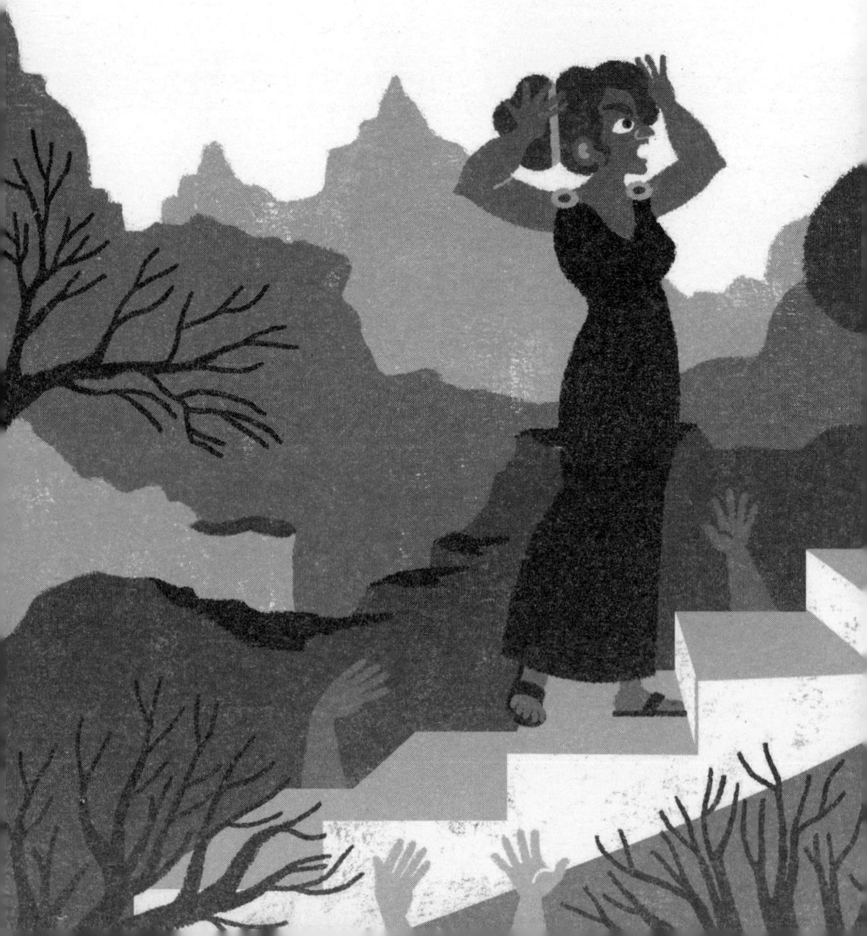

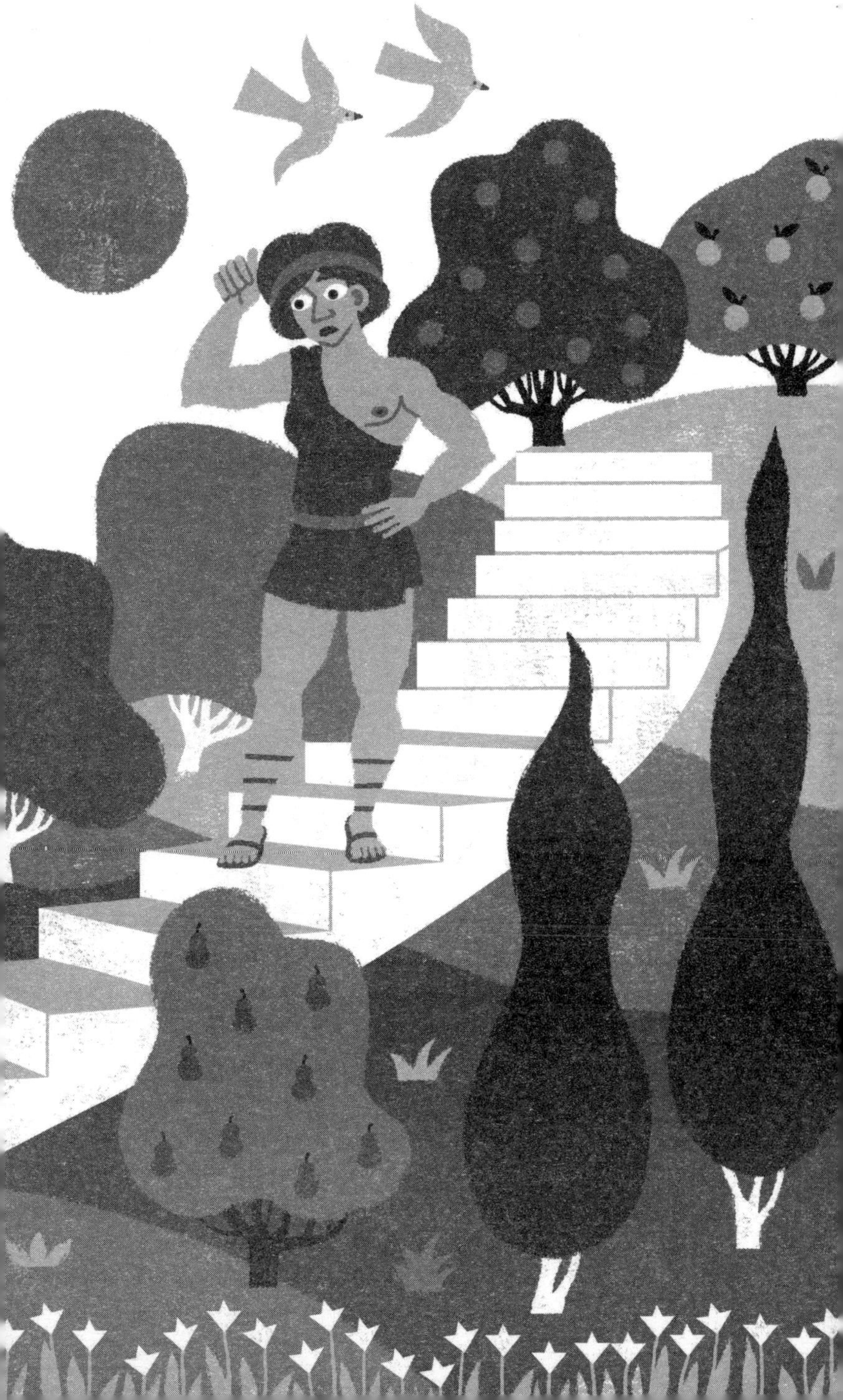

EROS AND PSYCHE

They're very happy together, so long
as she does what he wants.

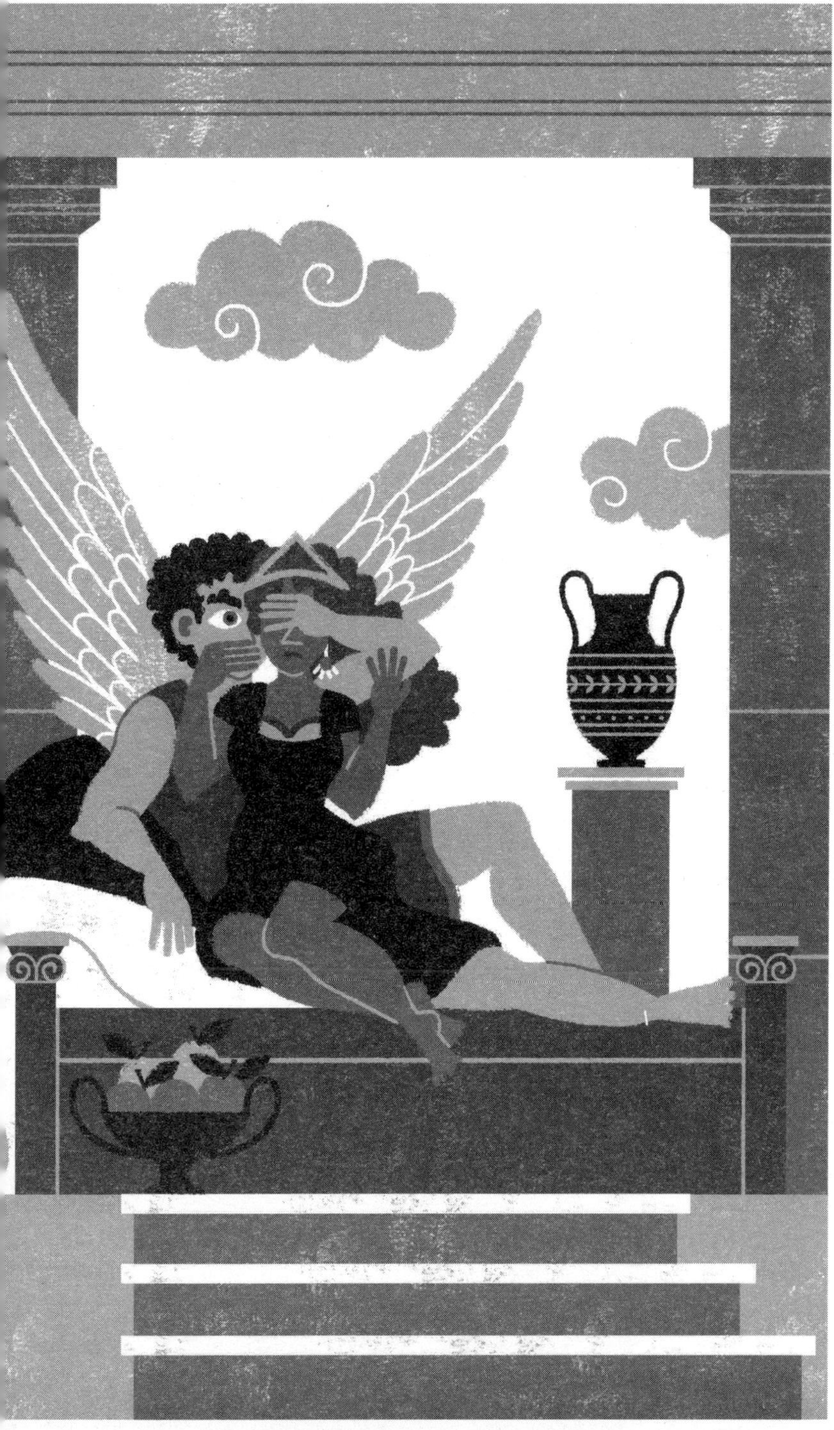

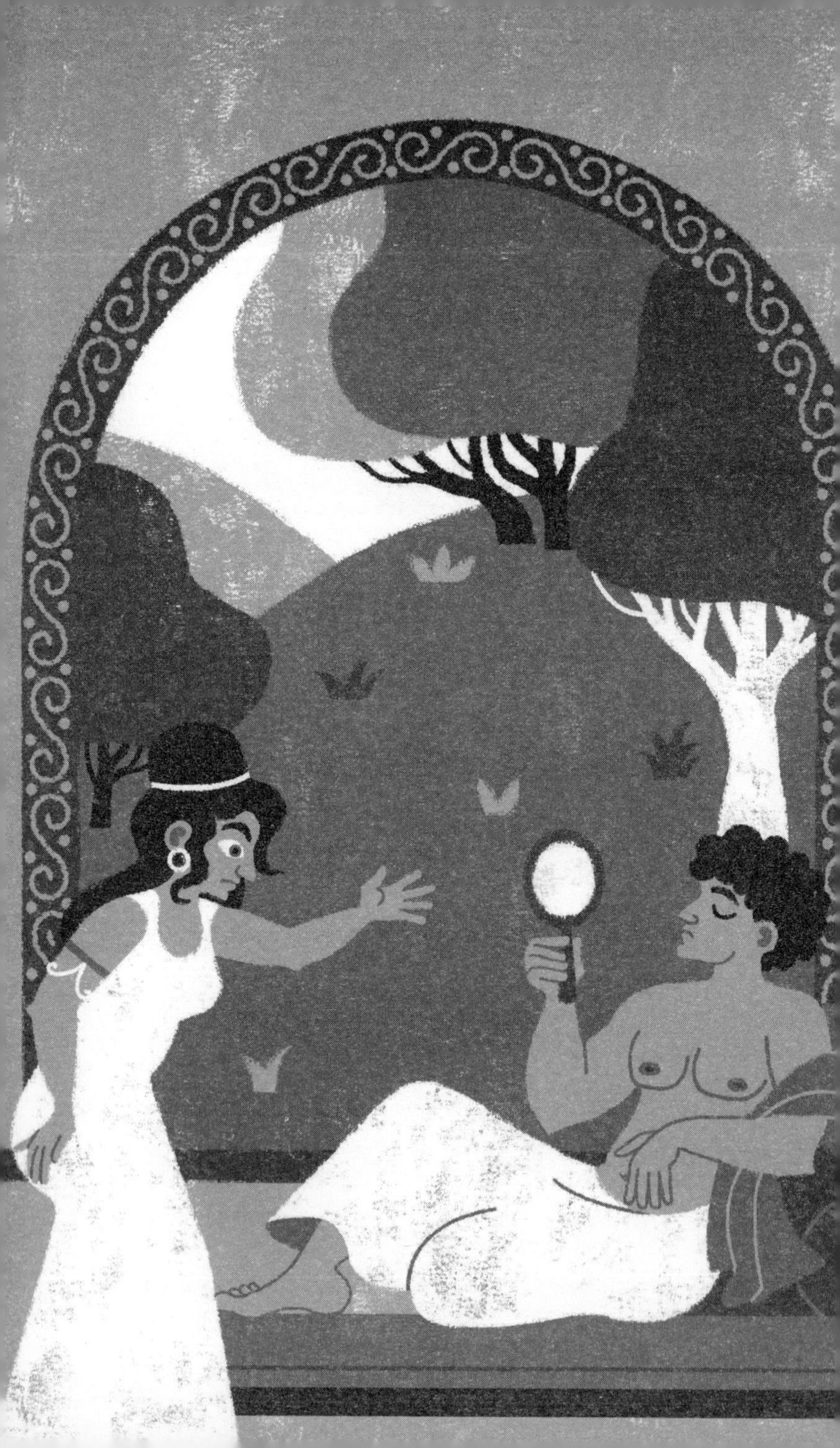

NARCISSUS AND ECHO

Echo was too clingy.

Echo was too chatty.

Echo just went on and on.

No wonder Narcissus preferred
playing with himself.

THE AMAZONS

Sexy, but troubling as a concept.

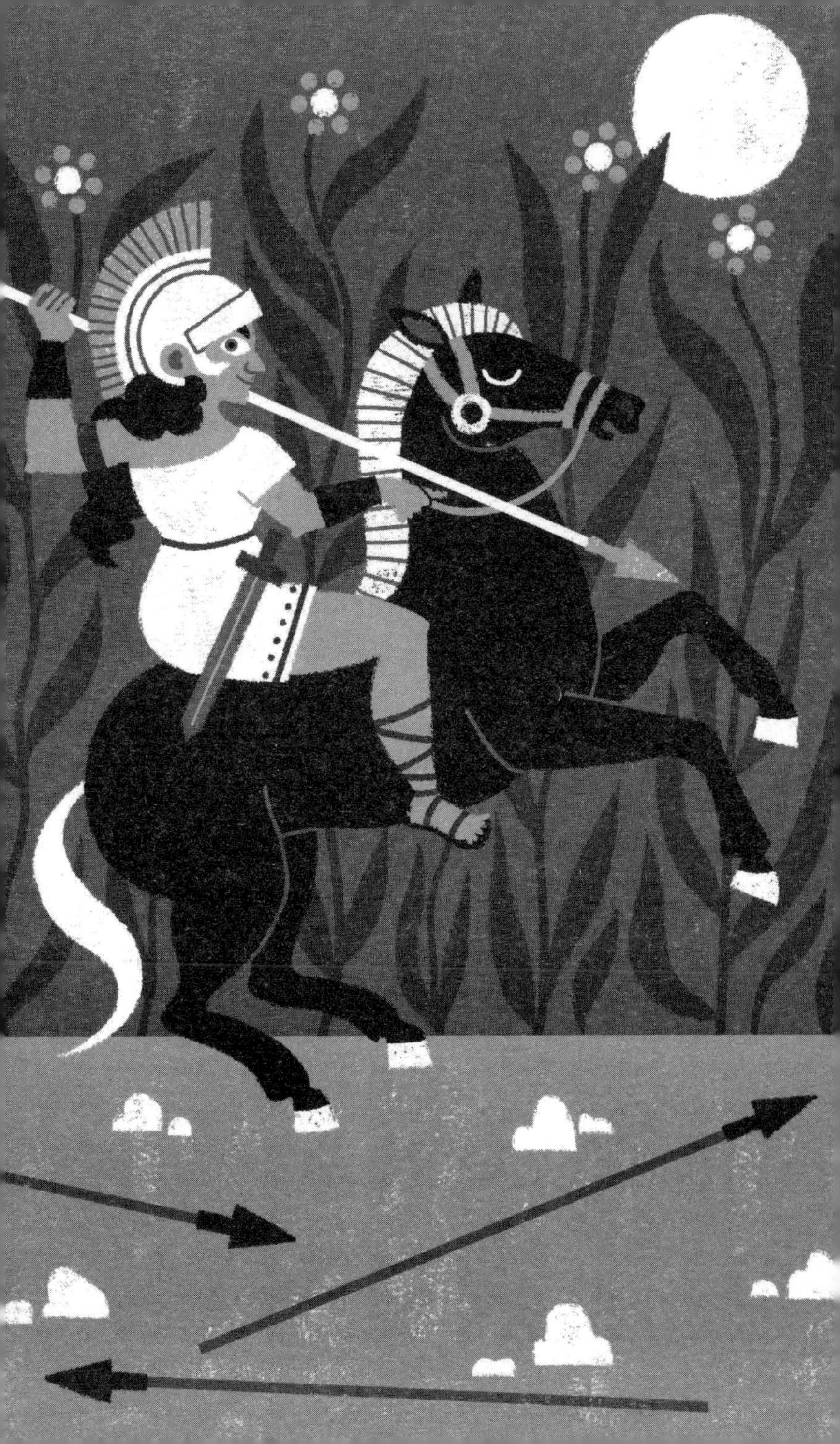

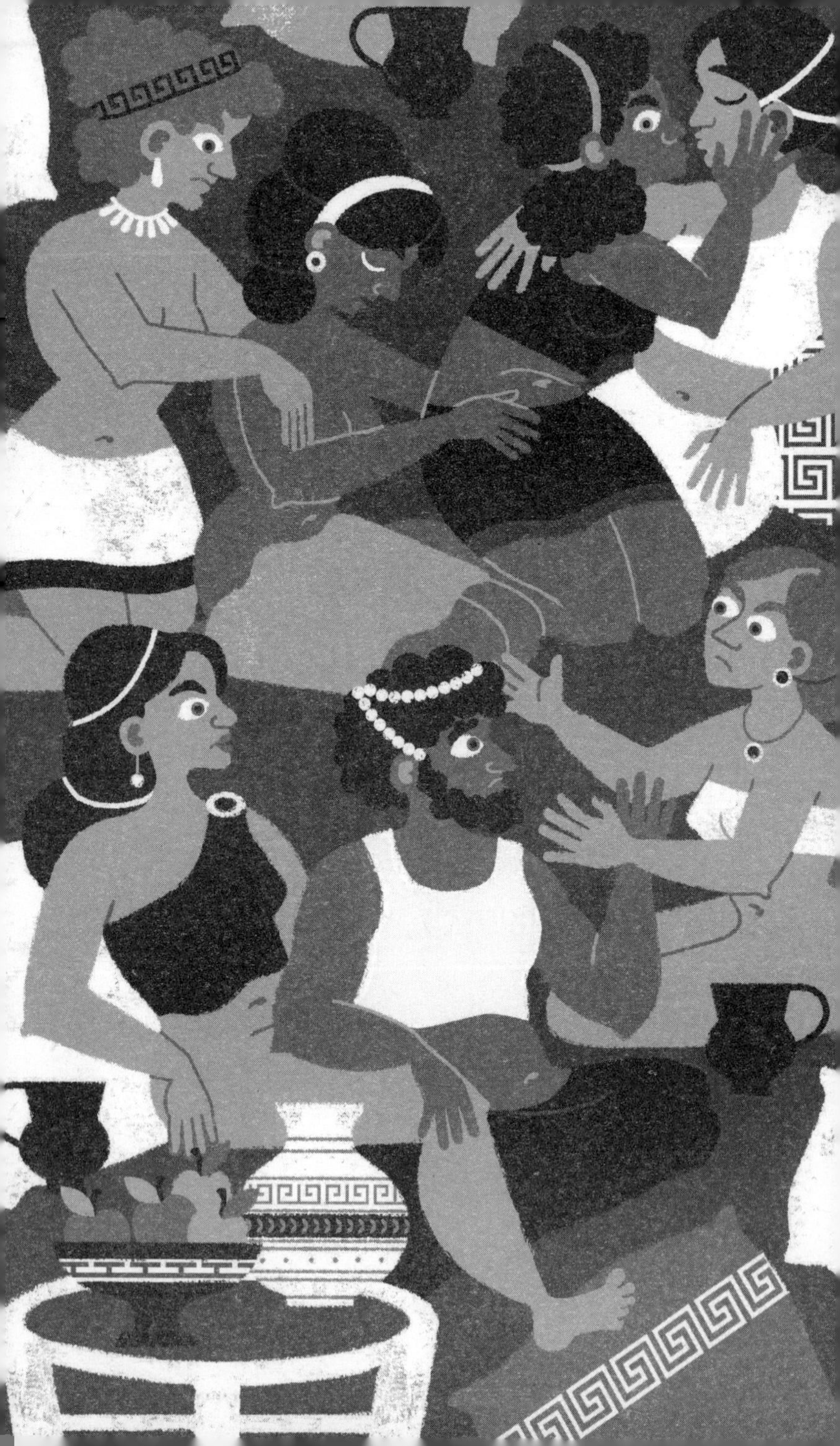

KING PENTHEUS MEETS A TRAGIC END

Pentheus put on a dress and lipstick
to watch a women-only orgy.

But something about him stuck out.

The women noticed,
and it all went horribly wrong from there.

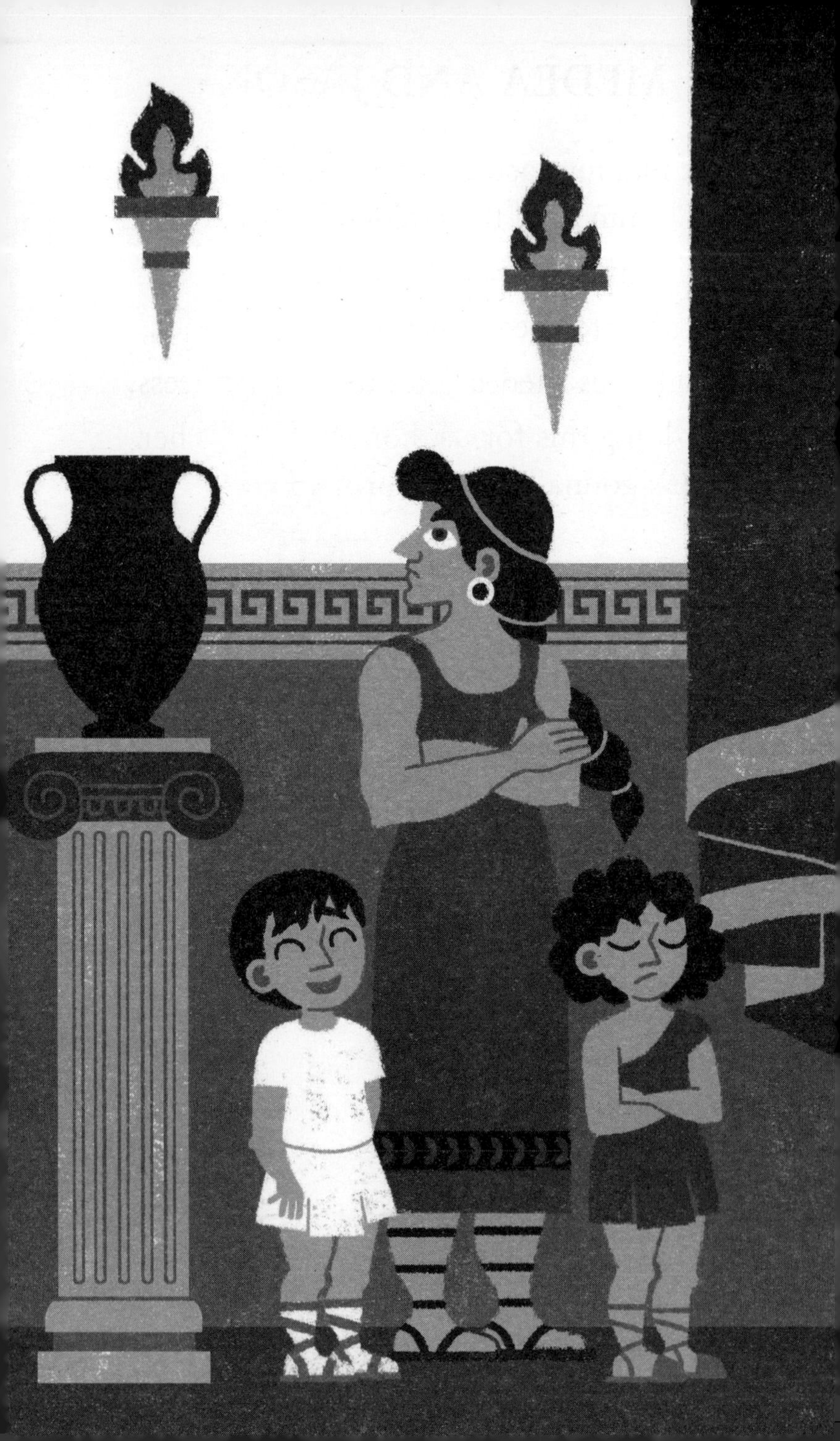

MEDEA AND JASON

After making Jason into a hero by helping
him steal the Golden Fleece
and win back his kingdom,
and after ten years of marriage and kids,
Jason leaves Medea for a teenage princess.
'I'm doing this for us, honey,' he tells her.
'It's gonna be great for the family.'

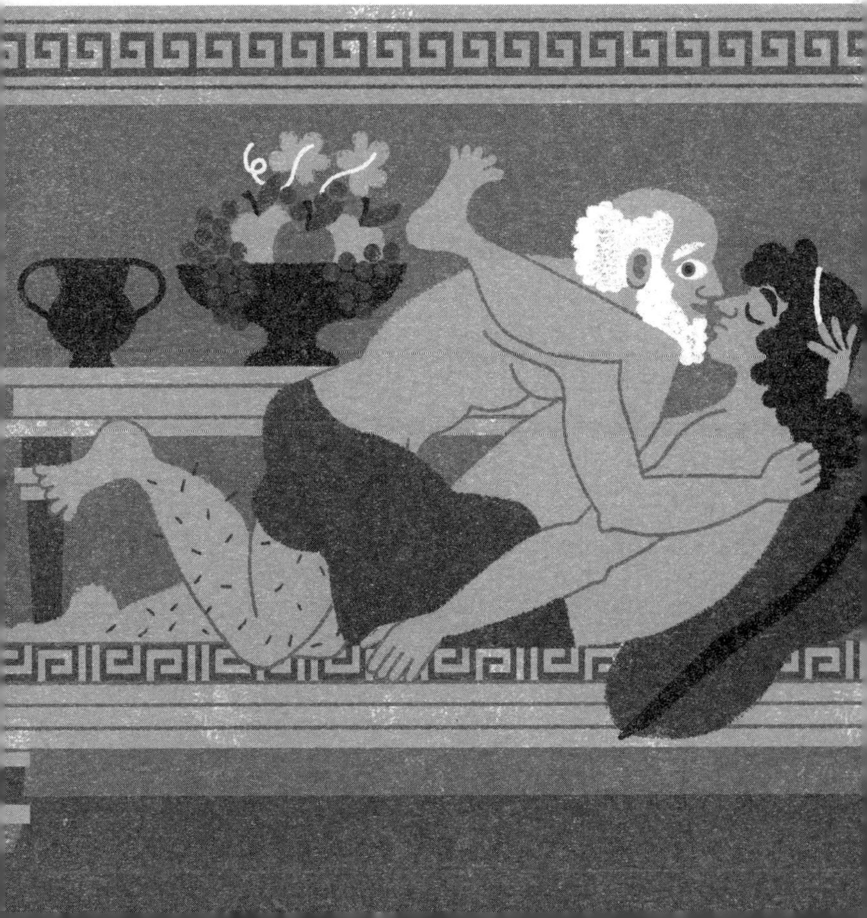

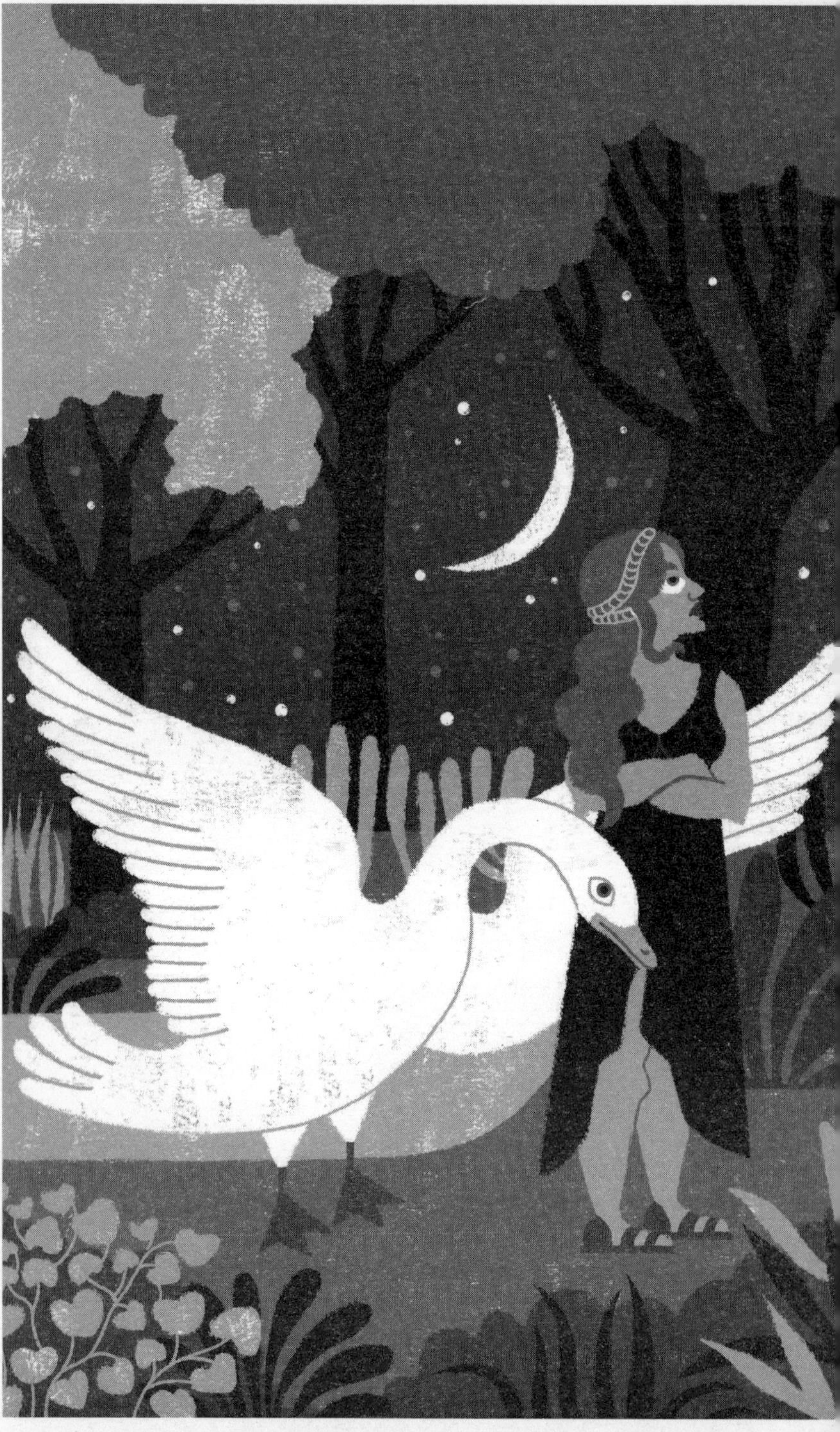

ZEUS AND LEDA

Zeus tried to find Leda's clitoris, he really did. But it was kind of difficult while pretending to be a swan.

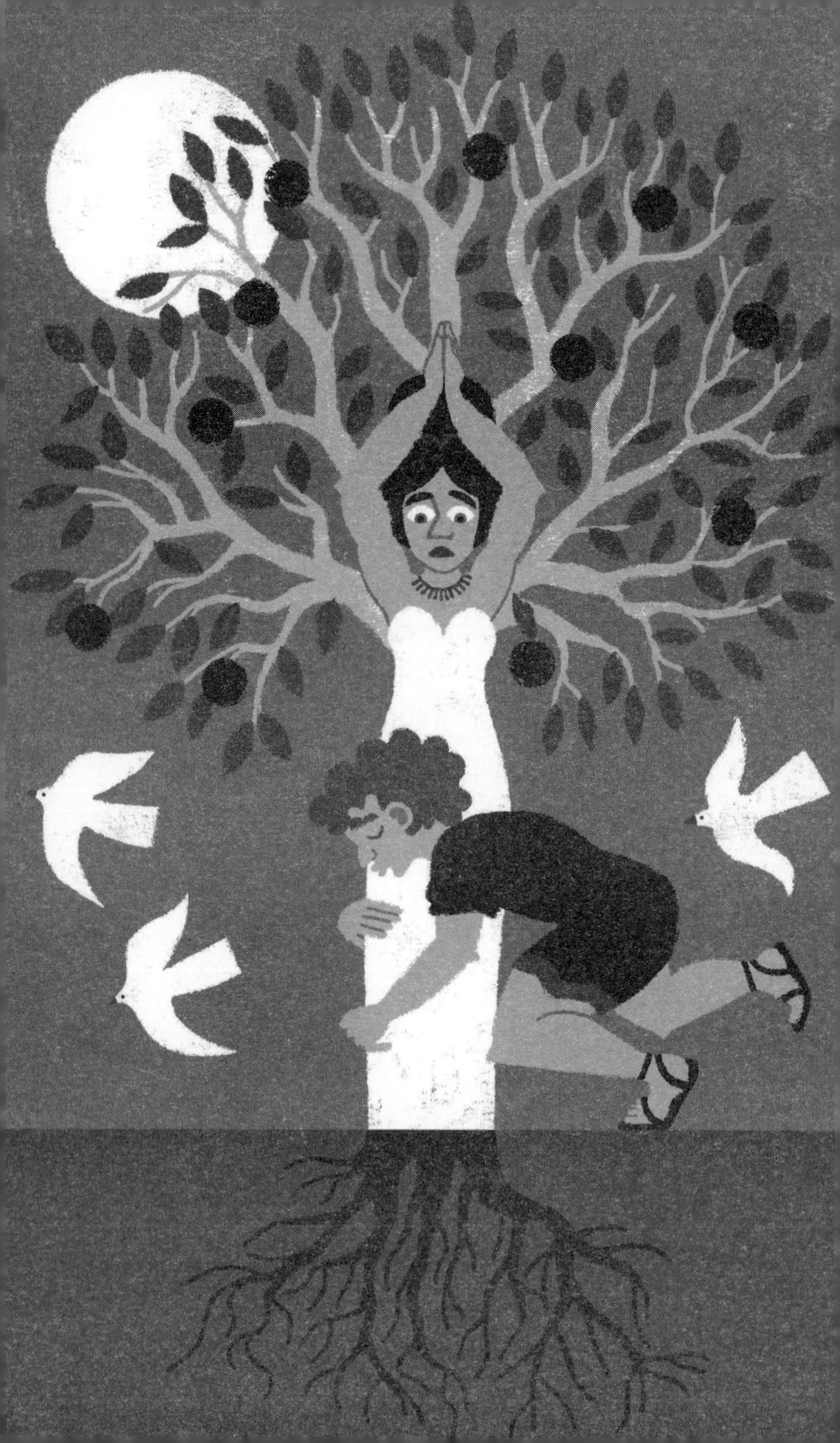

APOLLO LUSTS AFTER DAPHNE THE NYMPH

Daphne's dad wanted to protect his daughter
from the god,
but he couldn't find the chastity belt.

'I know,' he thought, 'I'll turn her into a tree.
That will do the trick!'

So, he did. And it did.

HERACLES

In a rage, Heracles crushed his wife
and children to death.

Afterwards, Heracles was sad.

Everyone felt sorry for him and agreed
that it wasn't his fault.

How could he help it?

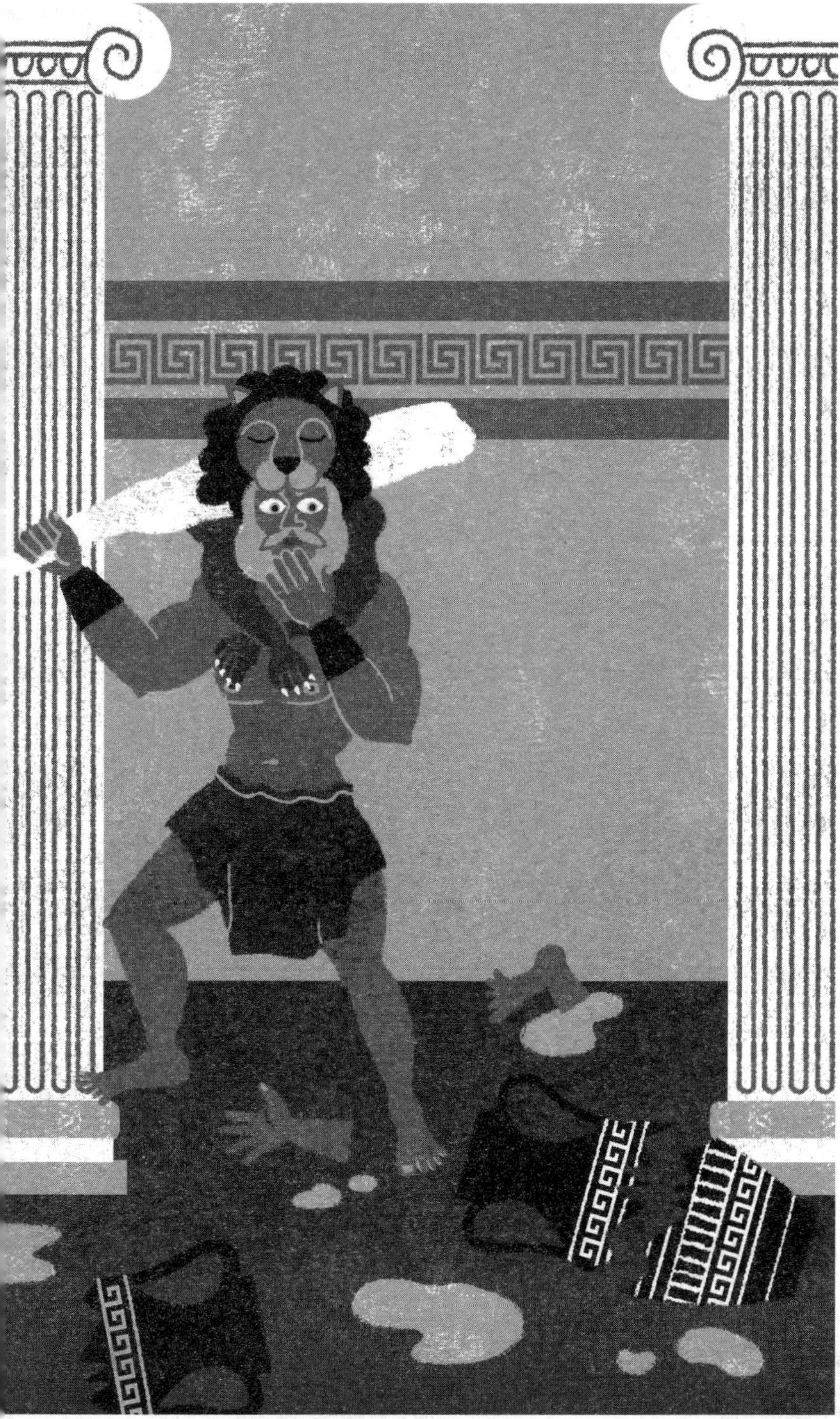

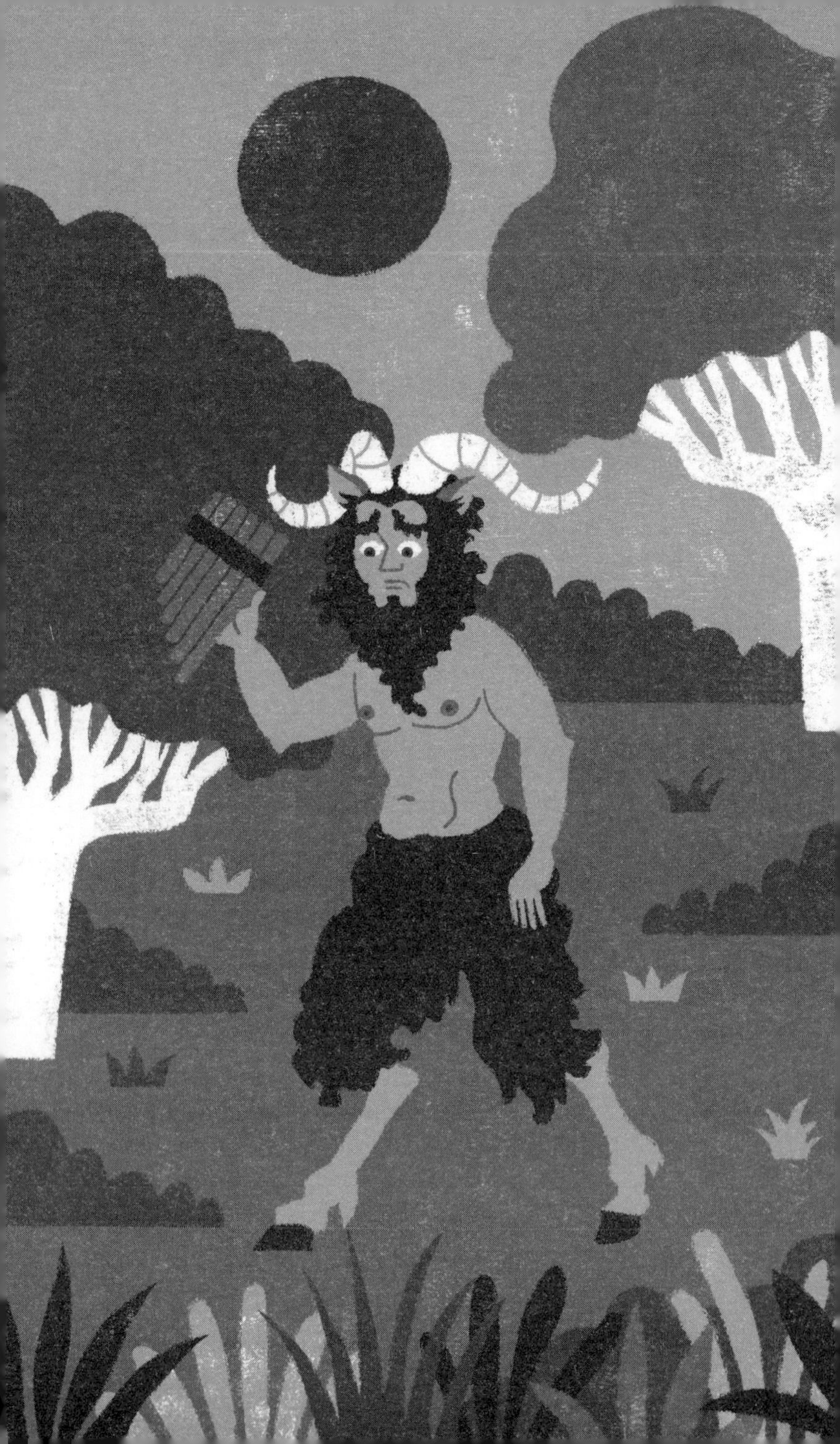

PAN AND SYRINX
THE NYMPH

Pan fancied Syrinx.

Syrinx said 'no'.

Pan did not understand 'no'.

So, Syrinx turned herself into a reed.

Pan still did not understand.

He cut the reed, and blasted Syrinx's spirit out.

Syrinx's spirit made a lovely 'o' sound.

So, Pan gave up on Syrinx and invented the panpipes instead.

Result!

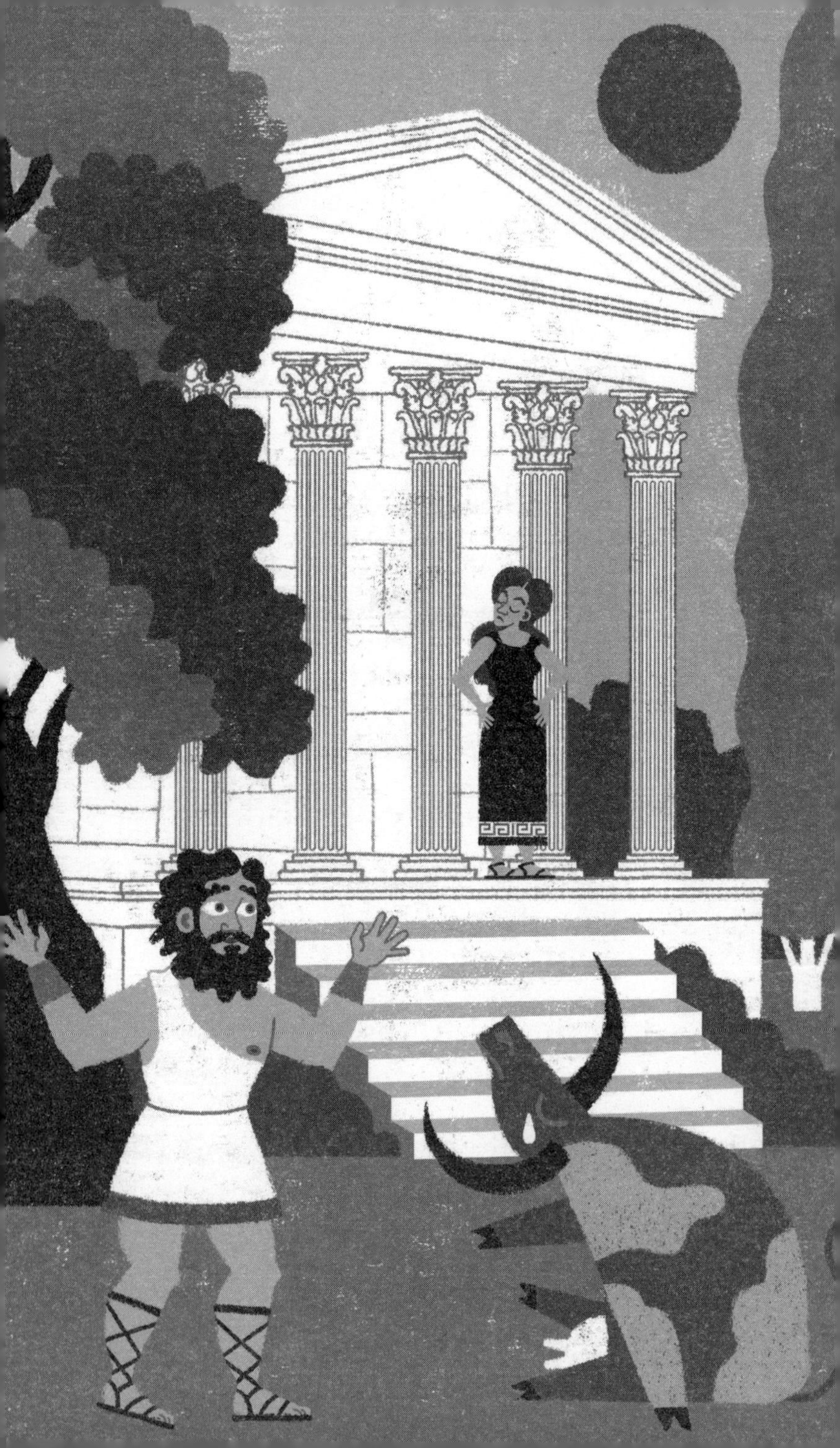

ZEUS AND IO

Zeus fancied Io, so he showered her in his love.

Hera found out and turned Io into a cow.

Io wasn't happy being a cow.

'I would totally turn you back into a woman,
I would,' Zeus said. 'I am, after all, the best,
the strongest, the most powerful of gods.
Of course, I am.

But the wife would kill me.'

HERACLES WINS HIPPOLYTA'S BELT

A man beats a woman in an arm wrestle.

That's the story.

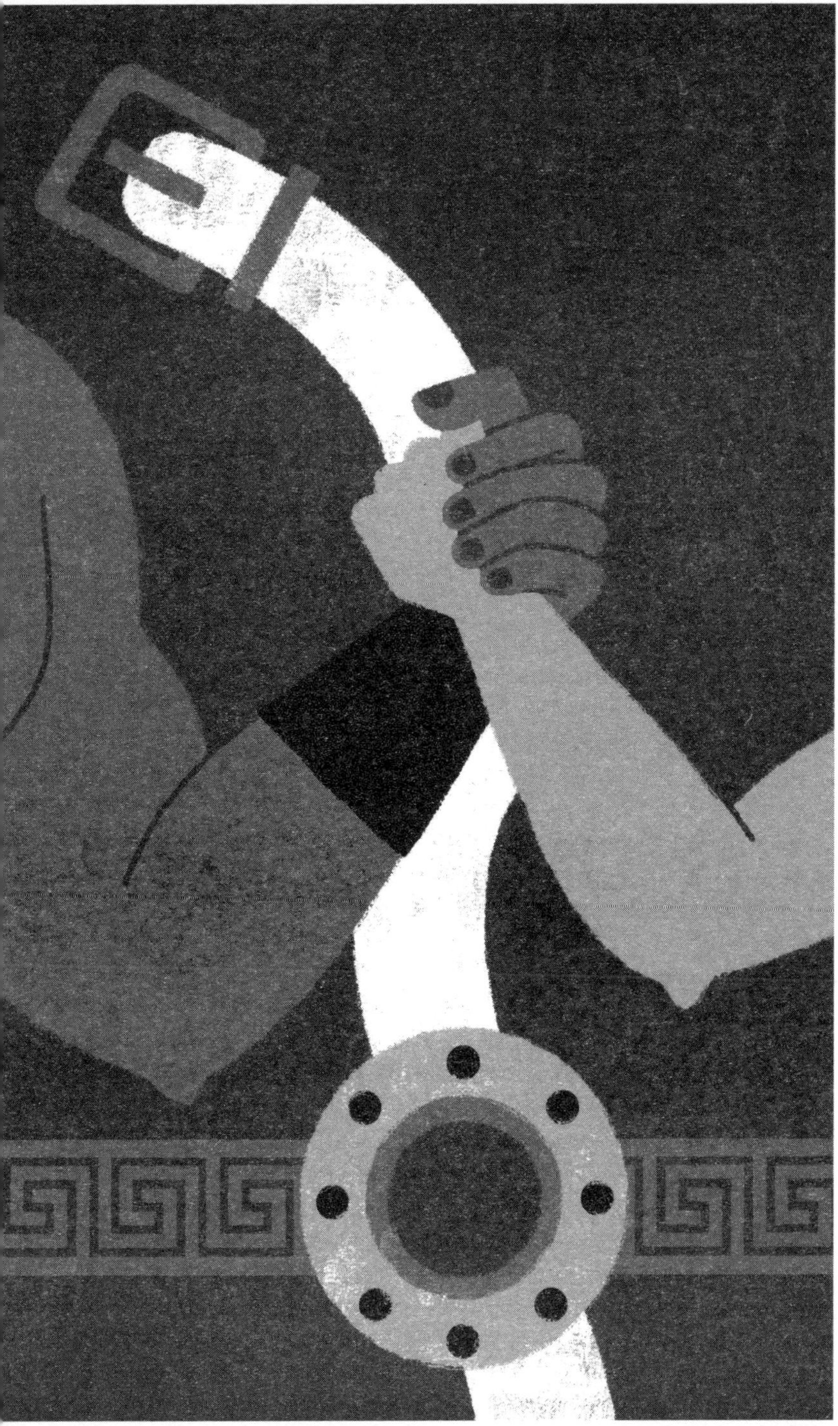

It's All Greek to Me!

Common Expressions for Everyday Life

TO OPEN PANDORA'S BOX:

Making trouble. A woman's exclusive.

AN ECHO:

Wife to husband: 'Are you even listening?'

'Listening?'

BEING A CASSANDRA:

Cassandra to husband: 'Let's ask for directions.'

Husband to Cassandra: 'I know where we're going.'

Cassandra to husband: 'If we don't ask, we'll get lost.'

Reader, they got lost.

TO HARP ON:

Only women do this. Men reiterate.

A SISYPHEAN TASK:

When you have to put down the loo seat.

Again.

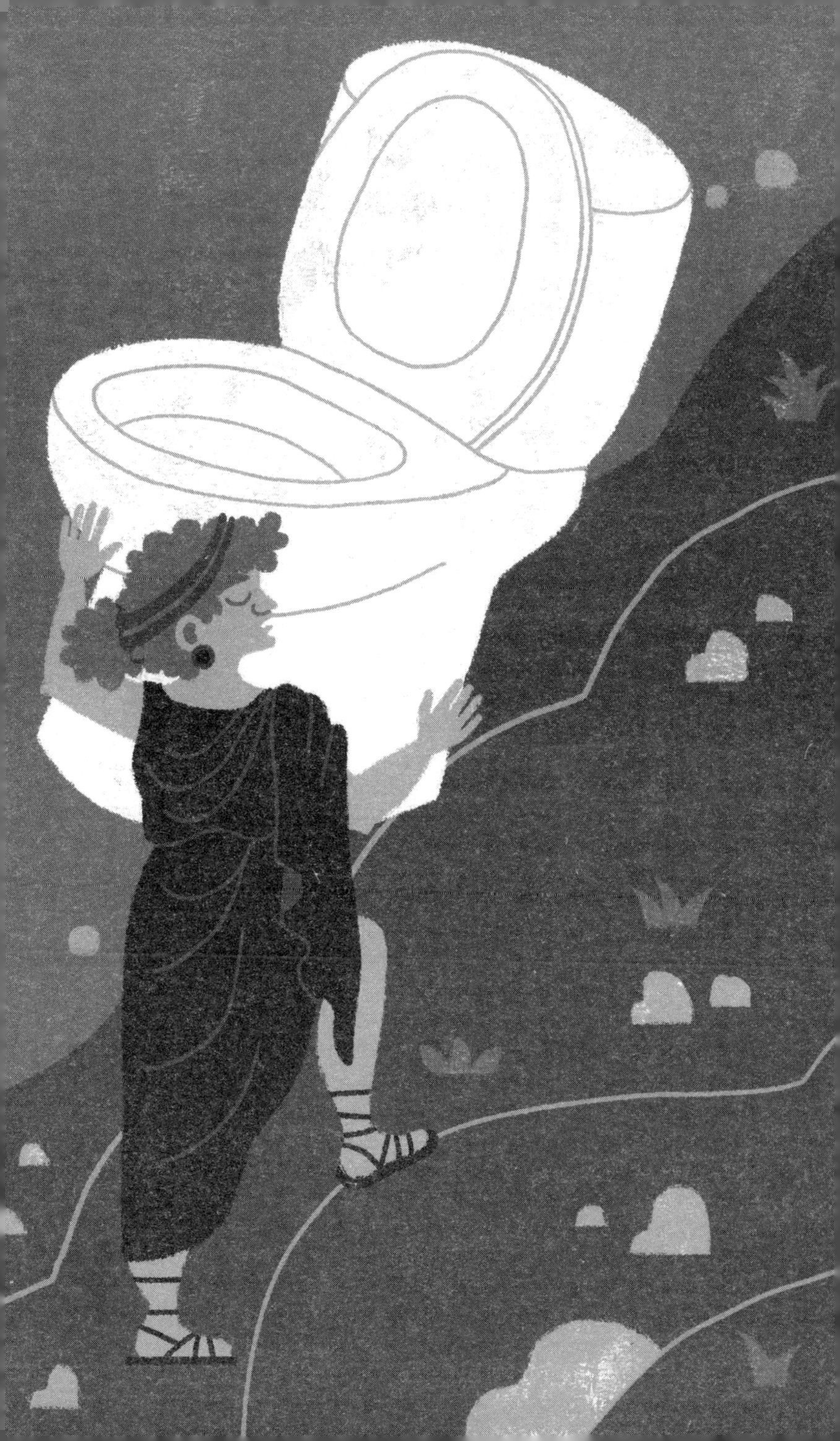

TO BE AN ADONIS:

A compliment.

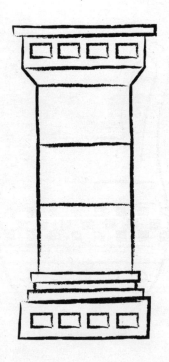

TO BE AMAZONIAN:

Not a compliment.

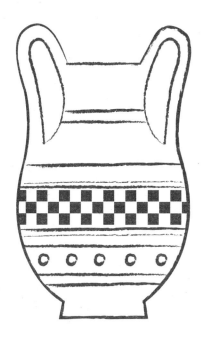

BEWARE OF GREEKS BEARING GIFTS:

Be careful when the nice man at the bar offers to show you his horse.

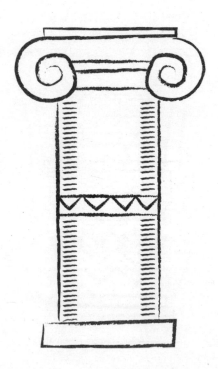

HYSTERIA:

Uniquely, female mental troubles that have nothing at all to do with men, like, ever.

FURY:

A feeling that helps you move on in life.

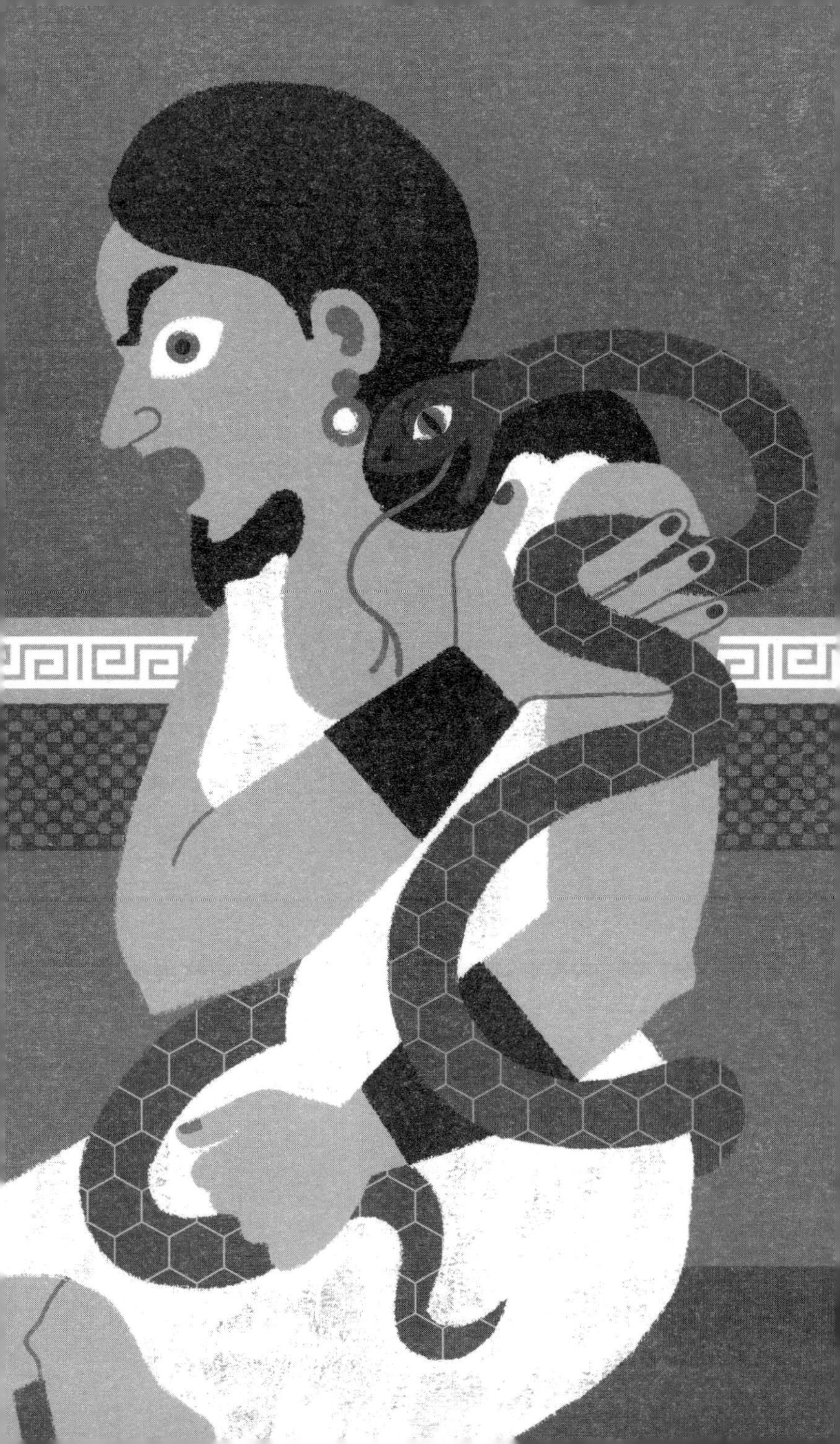

The
Trojan
War

TLDR: The Trojan War – Mostly Boring for Everyone Involved

Helen runs off with Prince Paris of Troy. Her Greek husband, Menelaus, isn't happy. He gathers his buddies to help him recapture Helen. This starts the siege of Troy, which lasts over ten years and involves a lot of sitting around outside, or inside, closed gates.

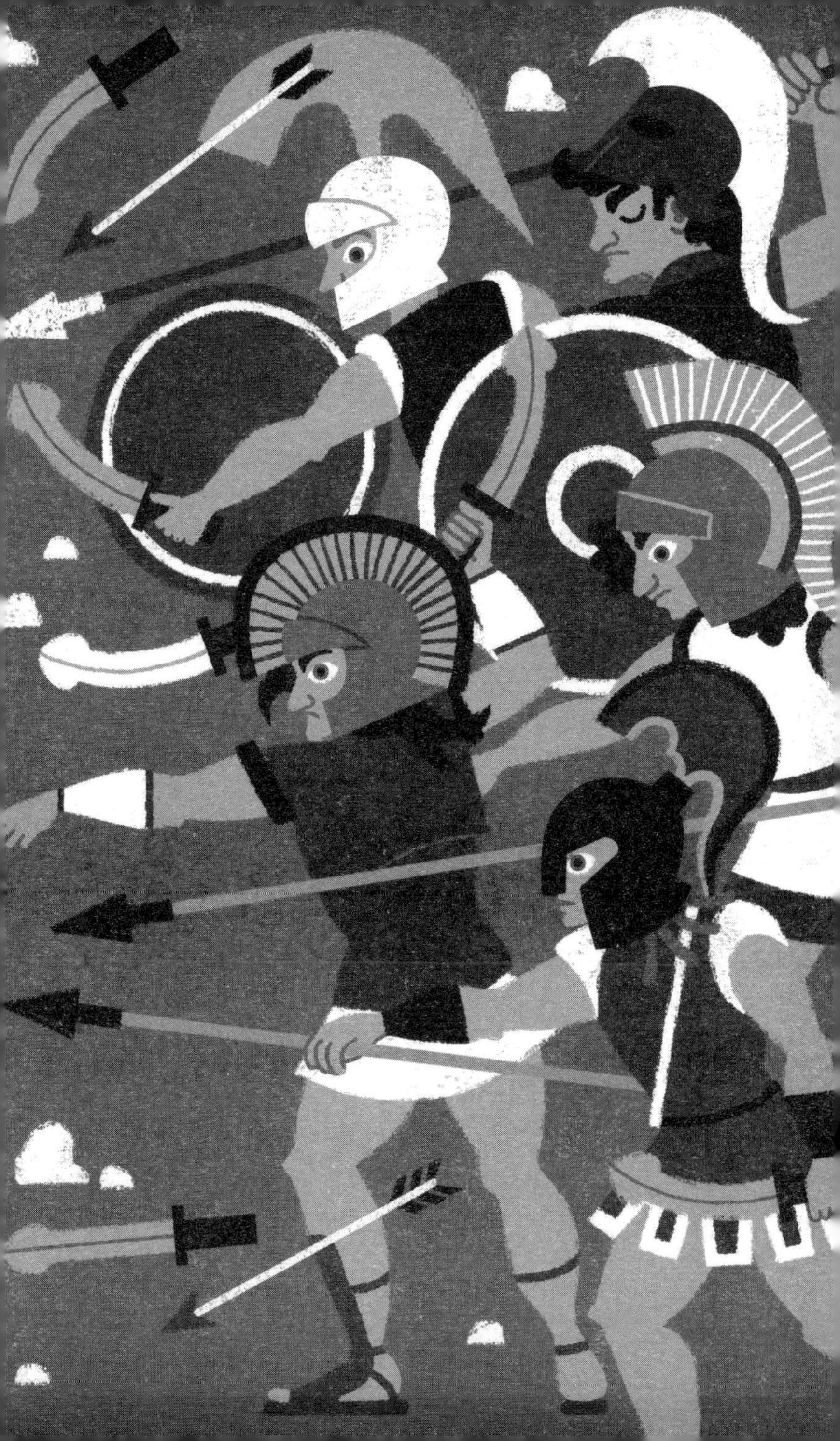

WHO'S WHO: TROJAN WAR AND THE WILLIAD

HELEN, QUEEN OF SPARTA

Wife of Menelaus. The Most Beautiful Woman on the Planet

The face that launched a thousand shits.
In fact, she just wanted to see Paris.

MENELAUS, KING OF SPARTA

Husband of Helen. Not the Most Beautiful Man on the Planet

Launches a thousand shits and starts a war because
Helen wanted to see Paris.

PARIS

Prince of Troy

Runs off with the most beautiful woman on
the planet, but turns out to be a wuss.

HECTOR

Paris' elder brother. Chief dick
of the Trojan army.

ACHILLES

Touchy Greek hero. Rapist.

PATROCLUS

Achilles' bestie and tent mate. Wink, wink.

BRISEIS

Achilles' slave and trophy girlfriend.

AGAMEMNON

Head of the Greek army. Rapist.

CASSANDRA

Princess of Troy. Annoyingly right about everything.

AJAX THE GREATER

Aka Big Ajax. Greek hero. Rapist.

ODYSSEUS

Greek hero. Rapist.

THE TROJAN HORSE

A ruse by the Greeks to capture Troy.

Weirdly enough, it succeeds.

THE BEAUTY CONTEST

Hera, Aphrodite, and Athena
     need to know:

Who is the fairest of them all?

Naturally, the judge is a man.

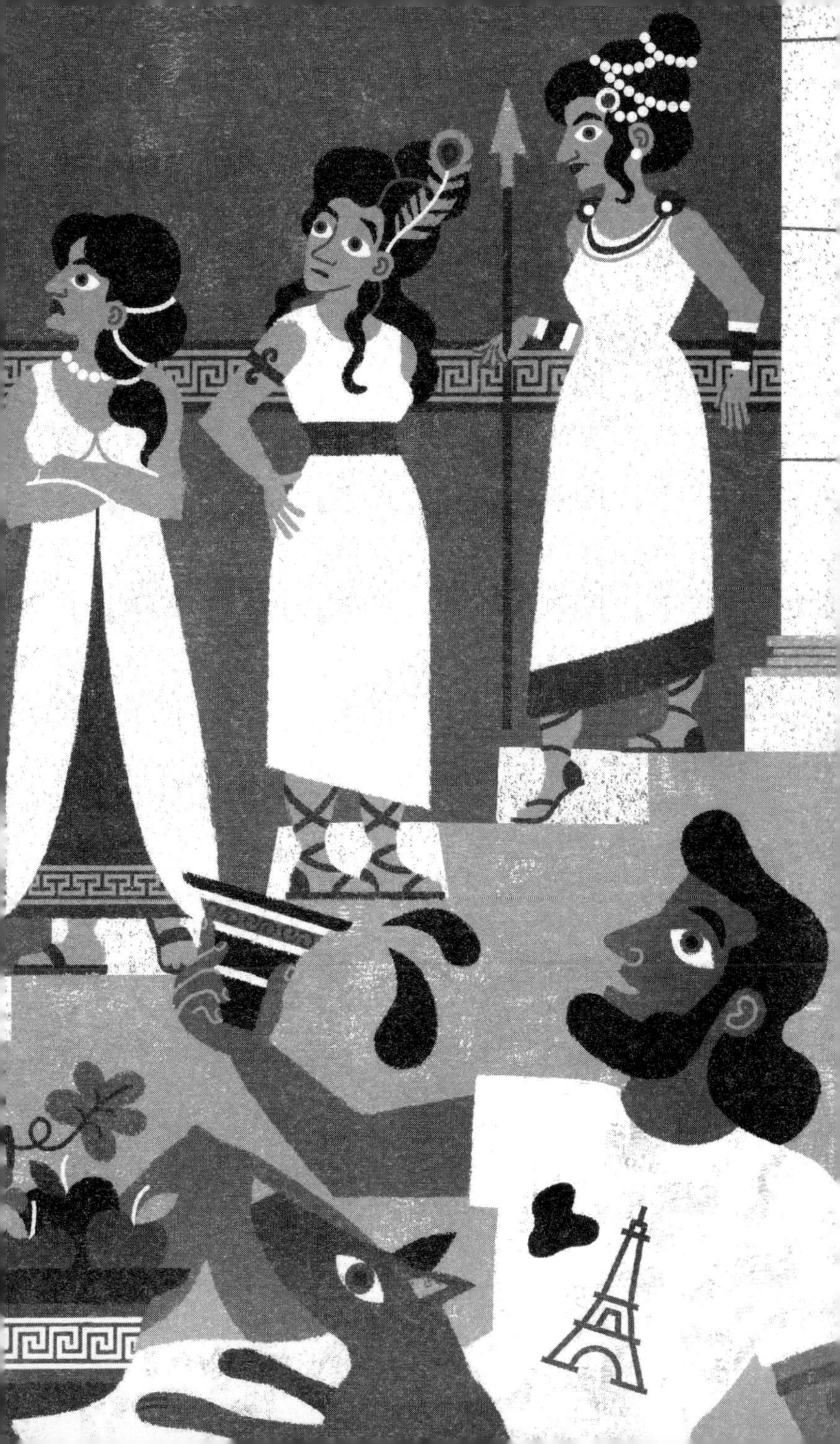

PRINCE PARIS OF TROY GETS TO JUDGE

Hera promises fame.
Athena promises glory.
Aphrodite promises Helen, the most beautiful woman on the planet.

Paris declares Aphrodite the winner.

Surprise, surprise.

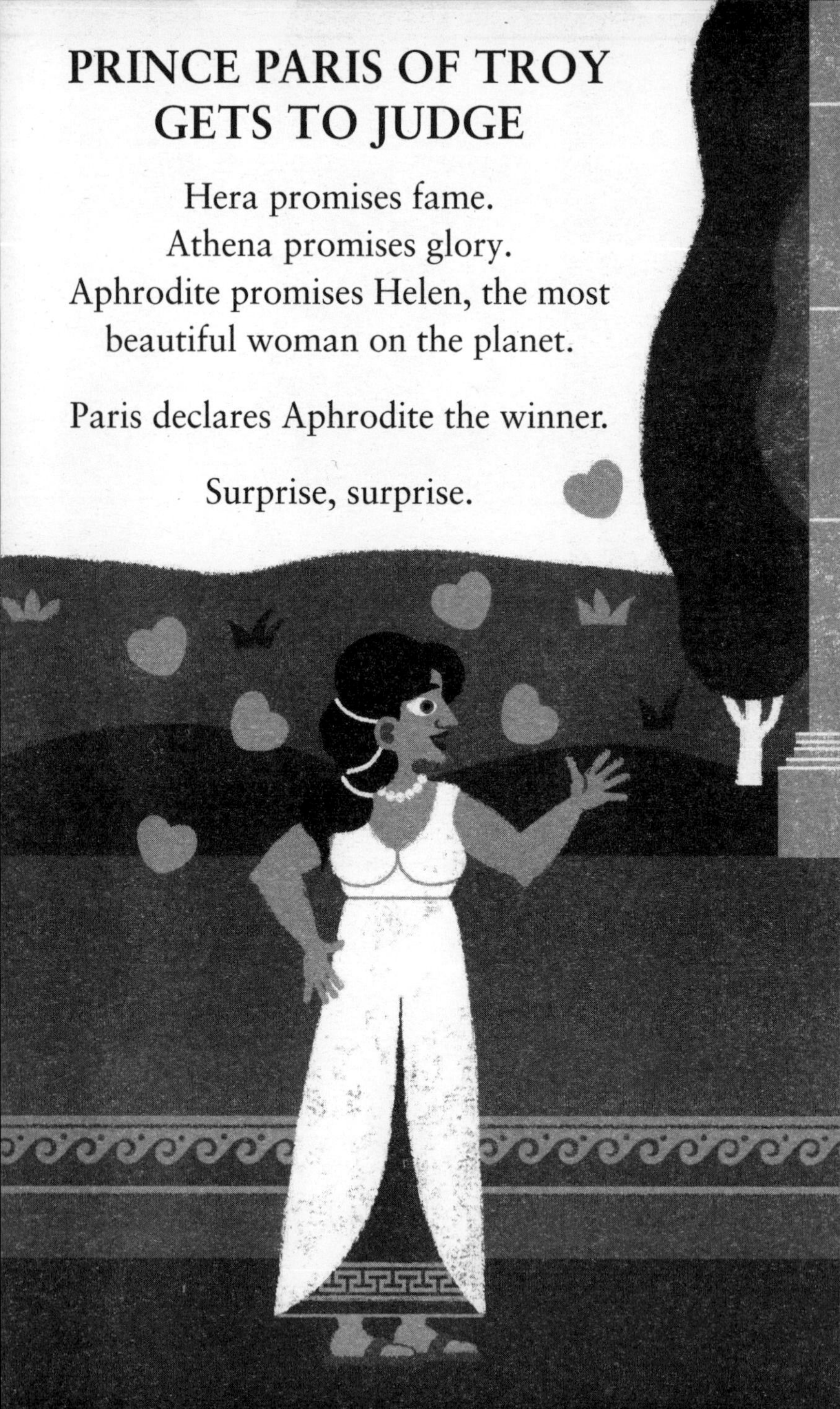

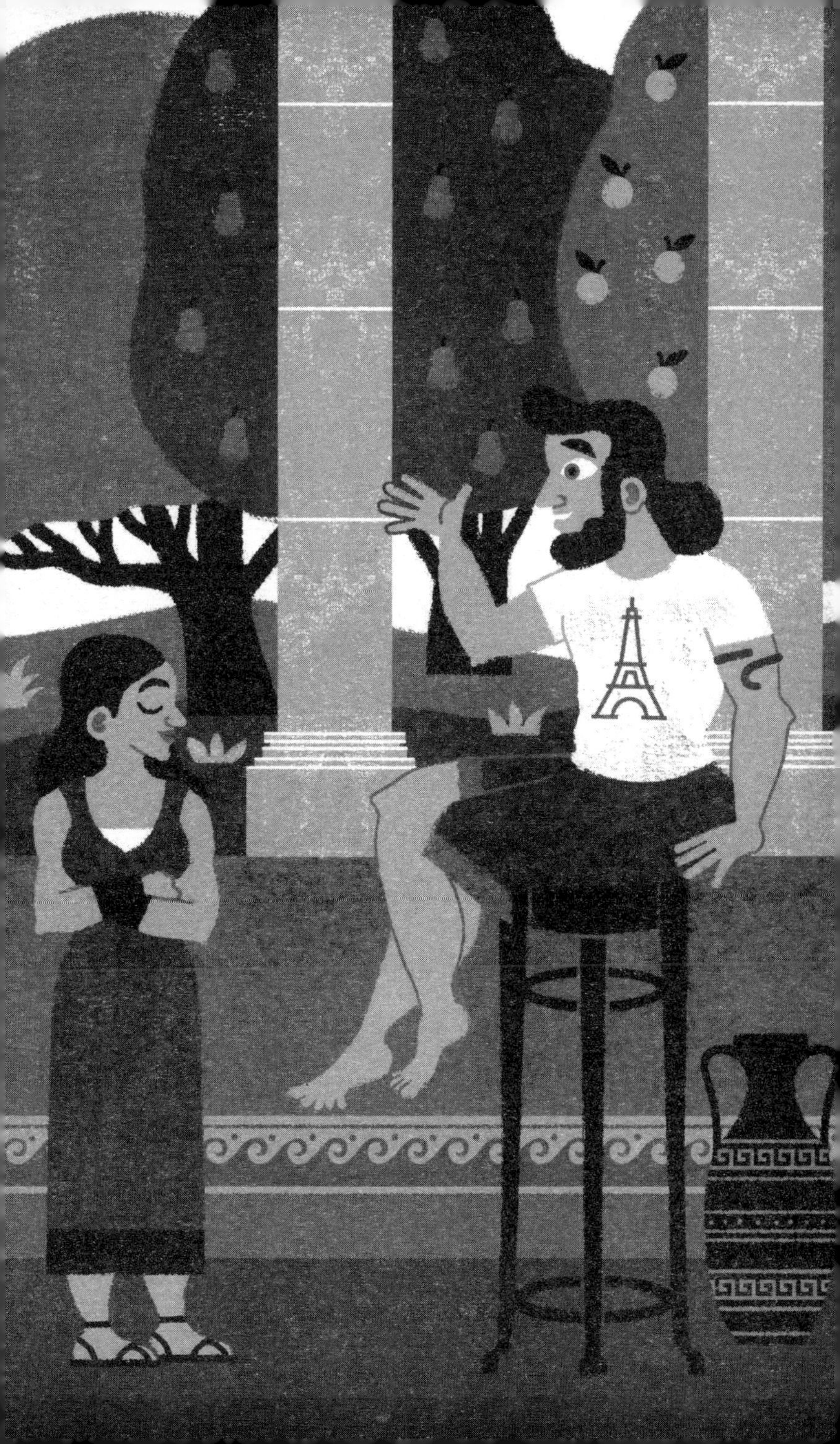

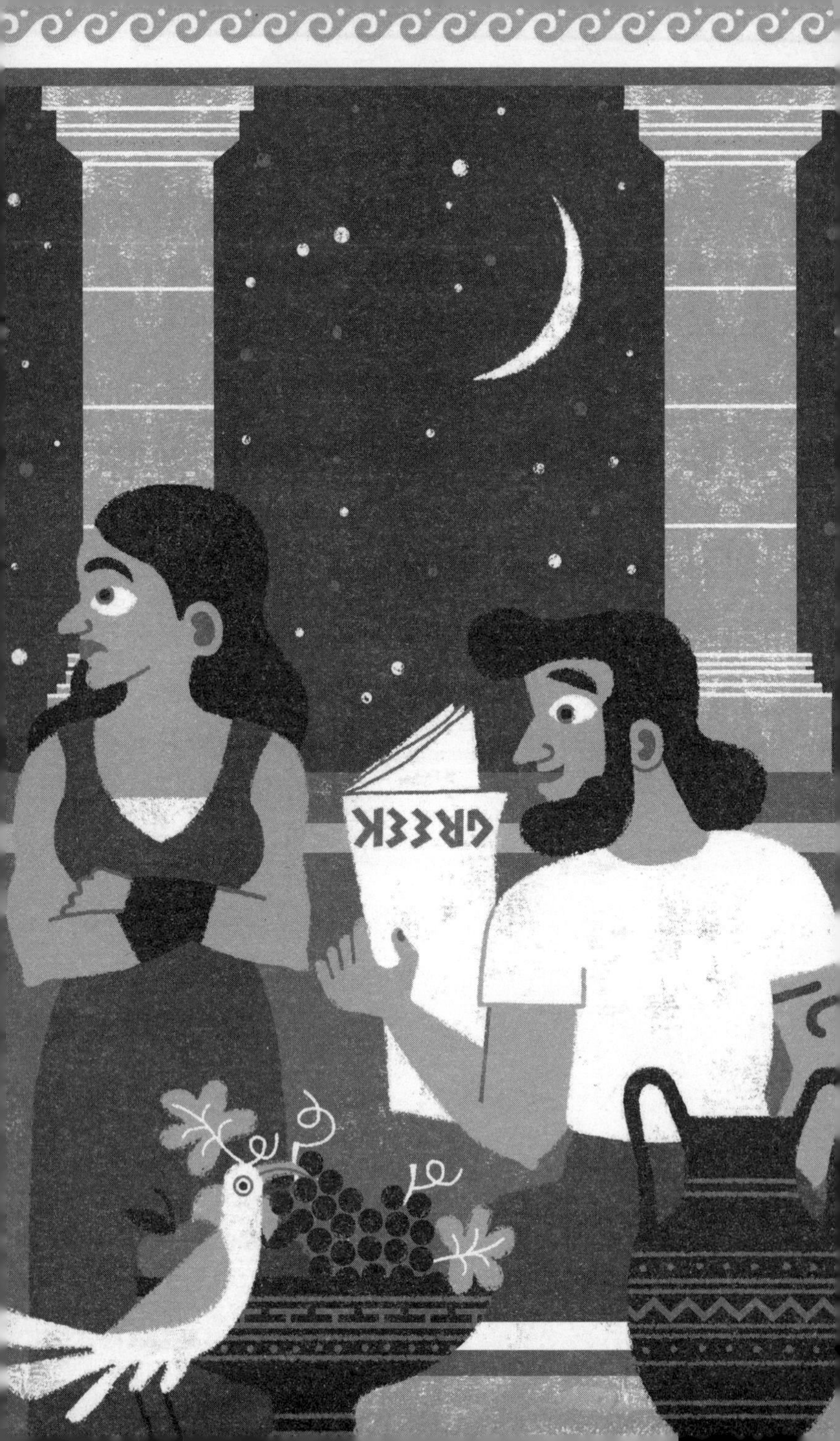
GREEK

PARIS ABDUCTS HELEN

Paris is less cultured than Helen expected.

MENELAUS DECLARES WAR ON TROY

They could just ask for Helen's opinion.

It might avoid a war.

But they don't.

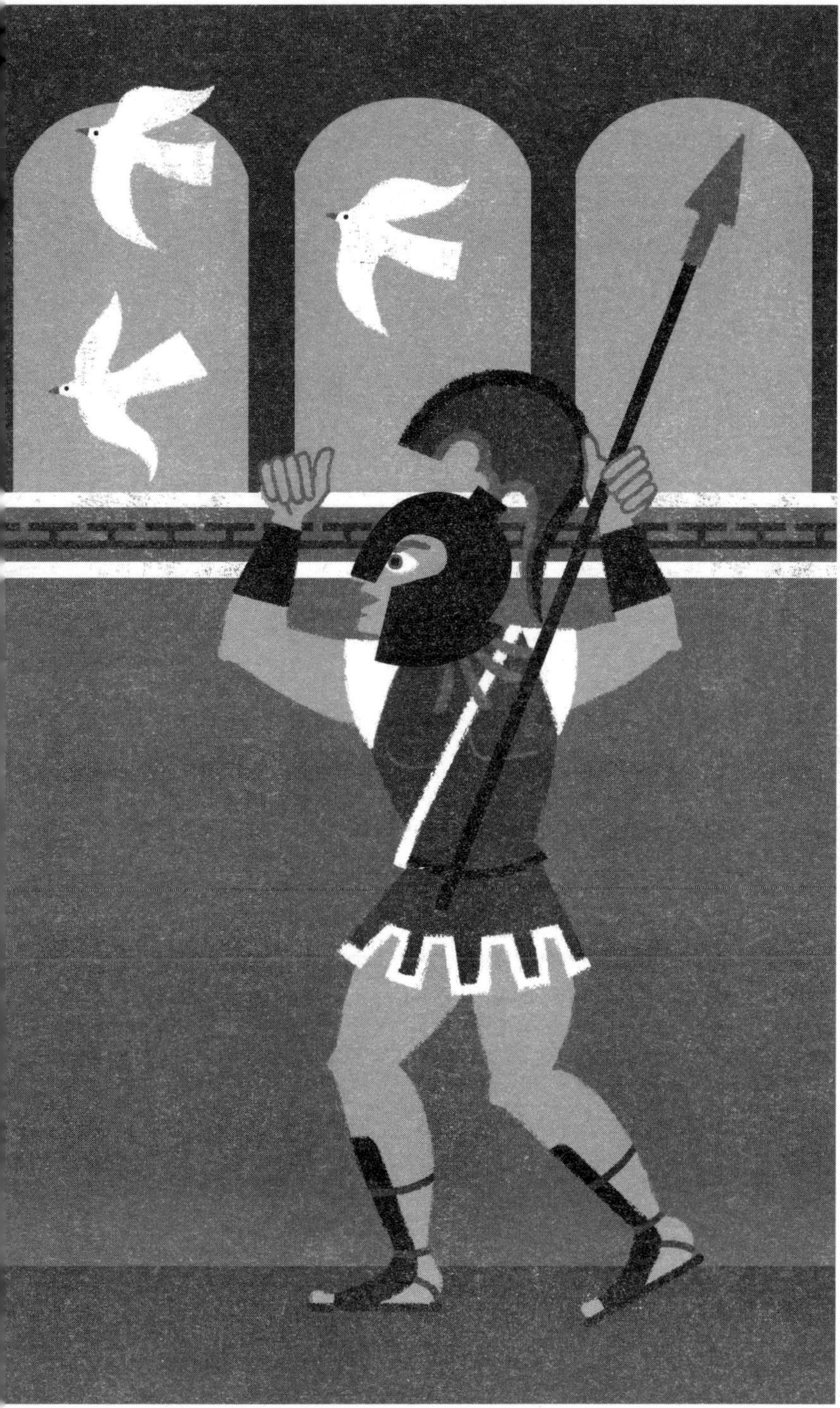

THE TROJAN WAR

Ten long years of dick waving, building up to
… THE WILLIAD.

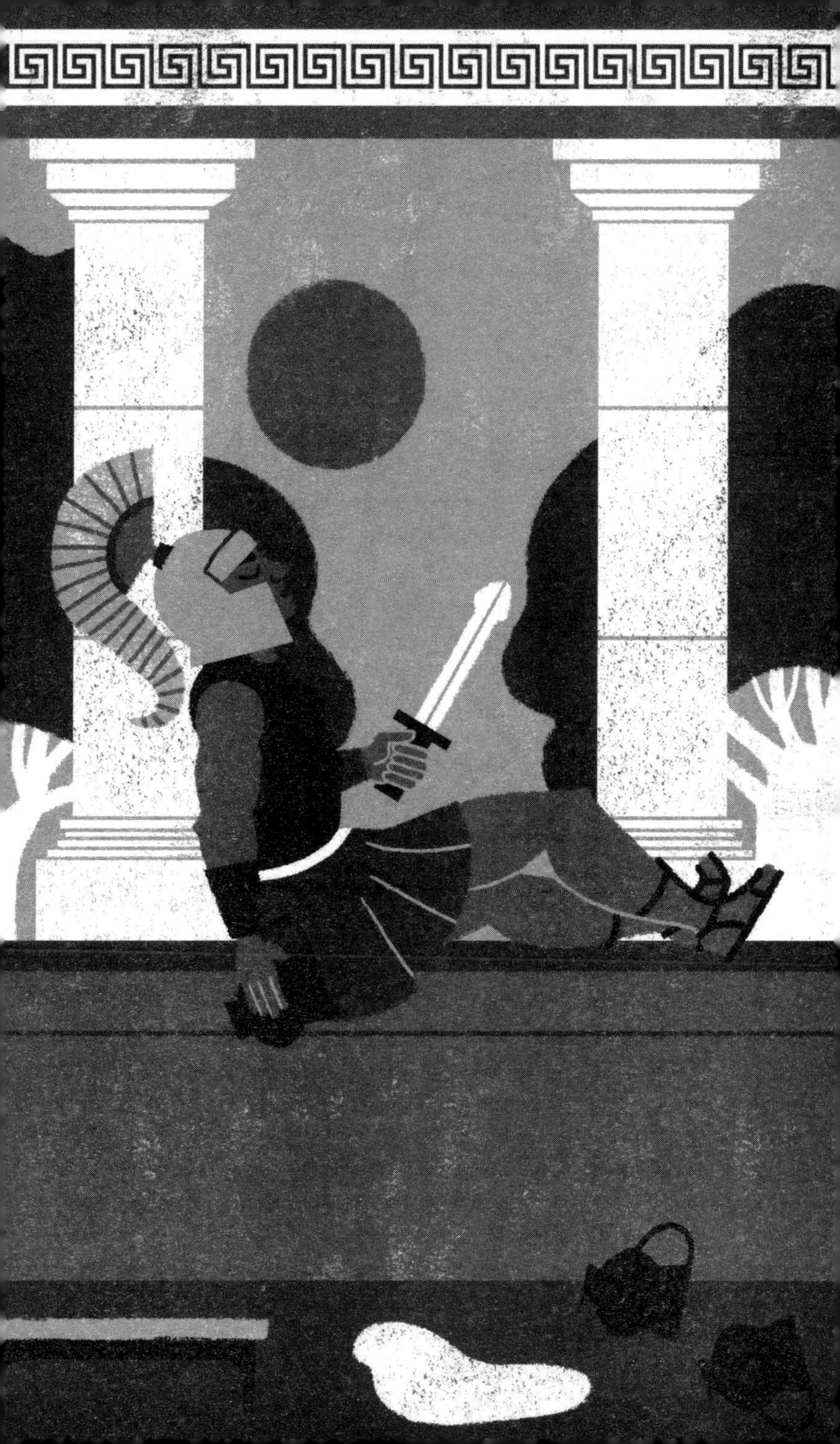

TLDR: The Williad

A really long poem in twenty-five books, all about the ninth year of the Trojan War. It's the story of men who have spent the past nine years of their lives waving their willies at each other deciding to wave their willies at each other some more. It's almost as if they never get tired of it. Sometimes the men have coffee together and agree that they should stop the willy-waving, really, but they don't quite know how. This makes it all very tragic.

The
Williad

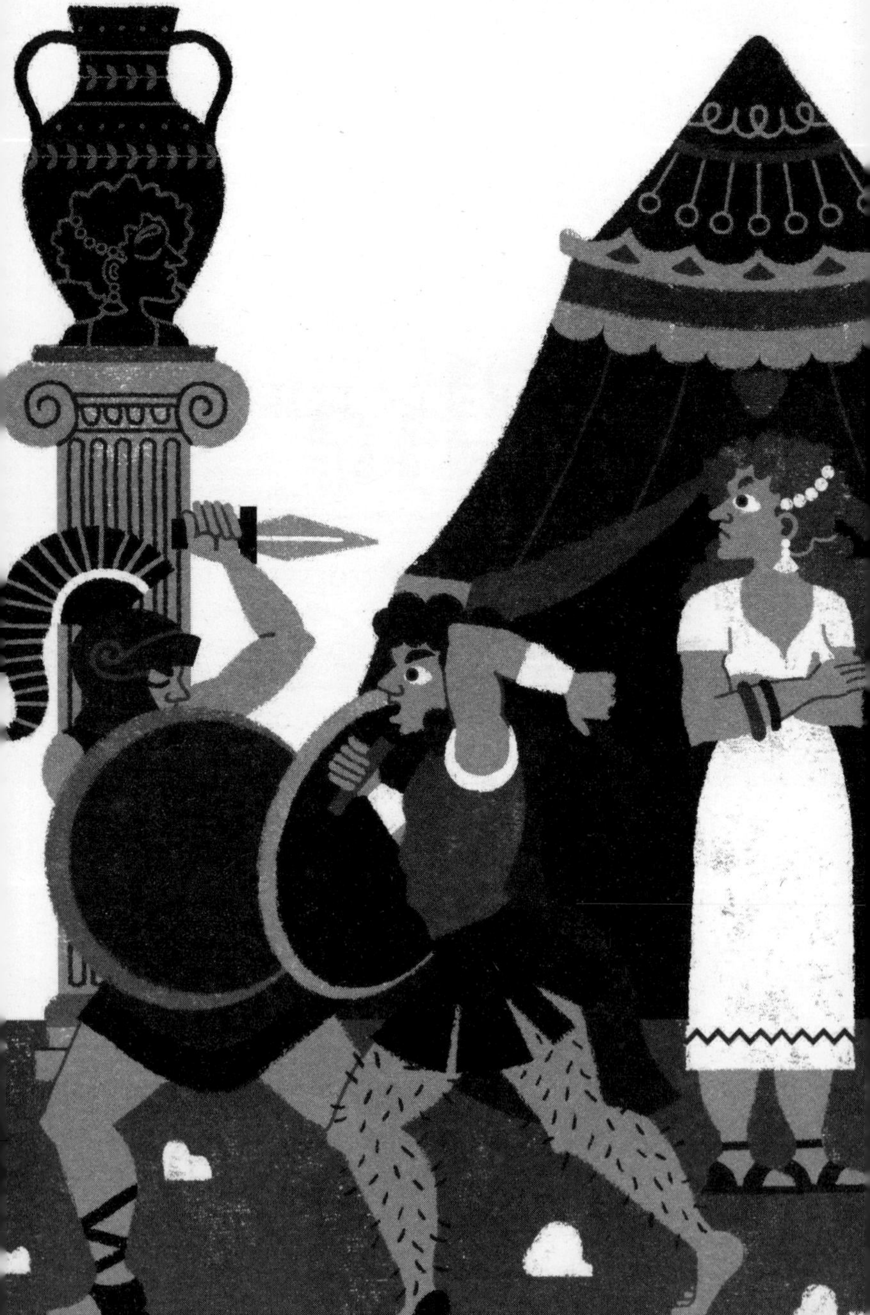

DISCORD IN THE GREEK CAMP

Agamemnon wants Achilles' trophy girlfriend.

Achilles doesn't want to give up his girlfriend.

They wave their willies at each other.

Agamemnon wins.

Achilles sulks and refuses to wave his willy
at the Trojans.

Nobody asks the girlfriend.

MEANWHILE IN TROY

'Beware the Greeks. We're all going to die,' says Cassandra.

Hysterical woman.

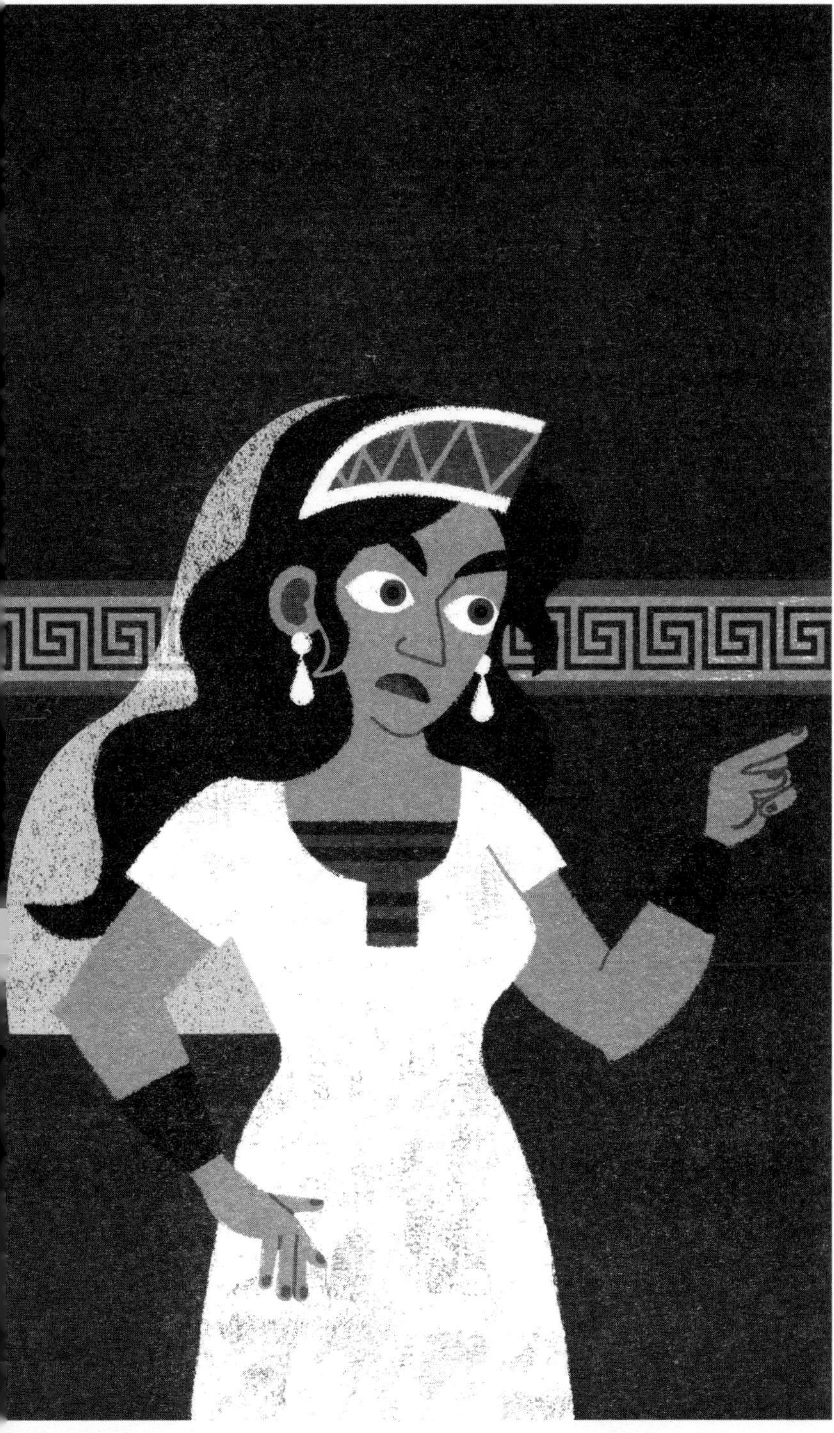

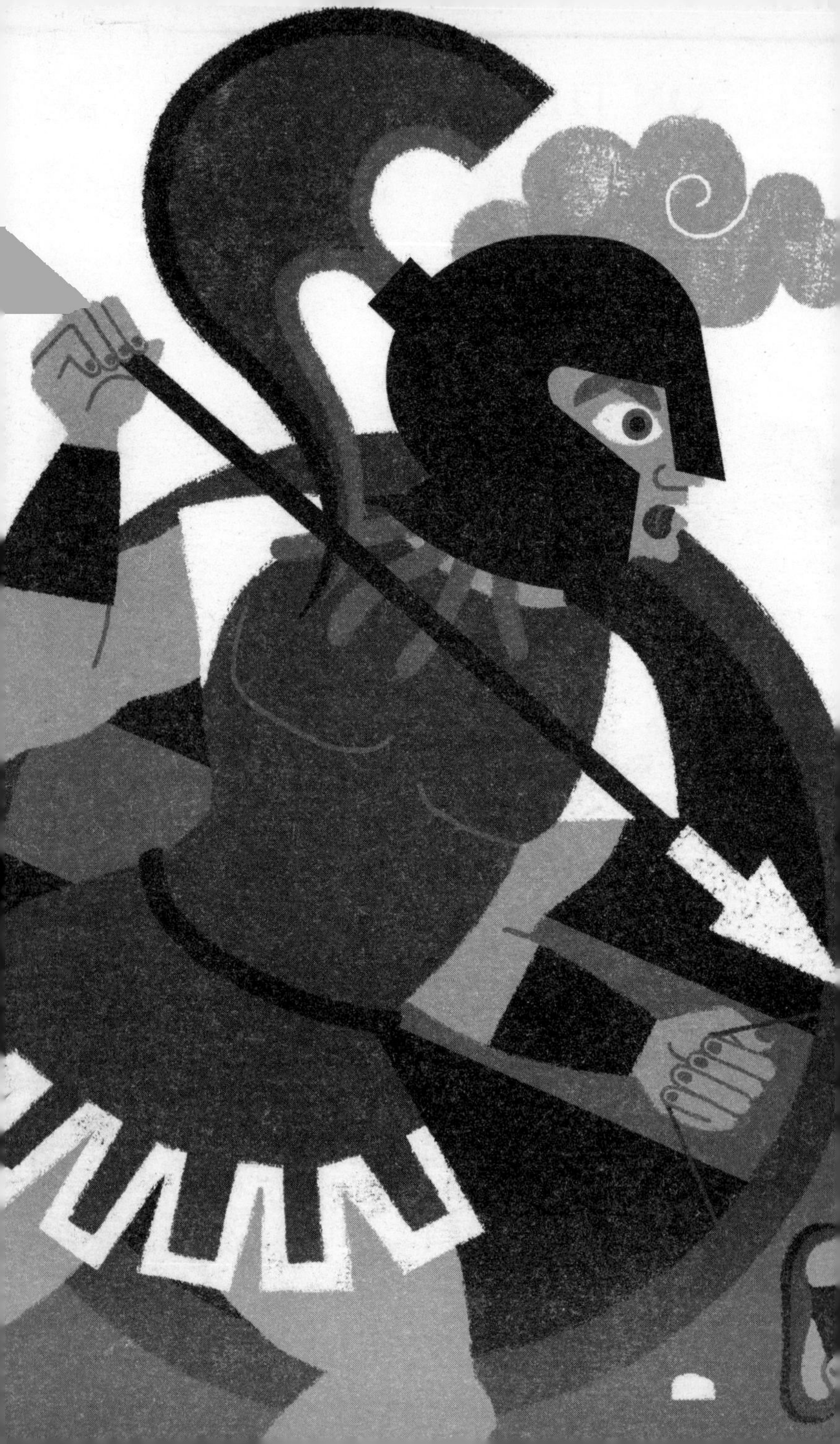

ON THE BATTLEFIELD

Menelaus waves his willy at Paris. Paris runs away. The battle starts up again. More willy-waving ensues.

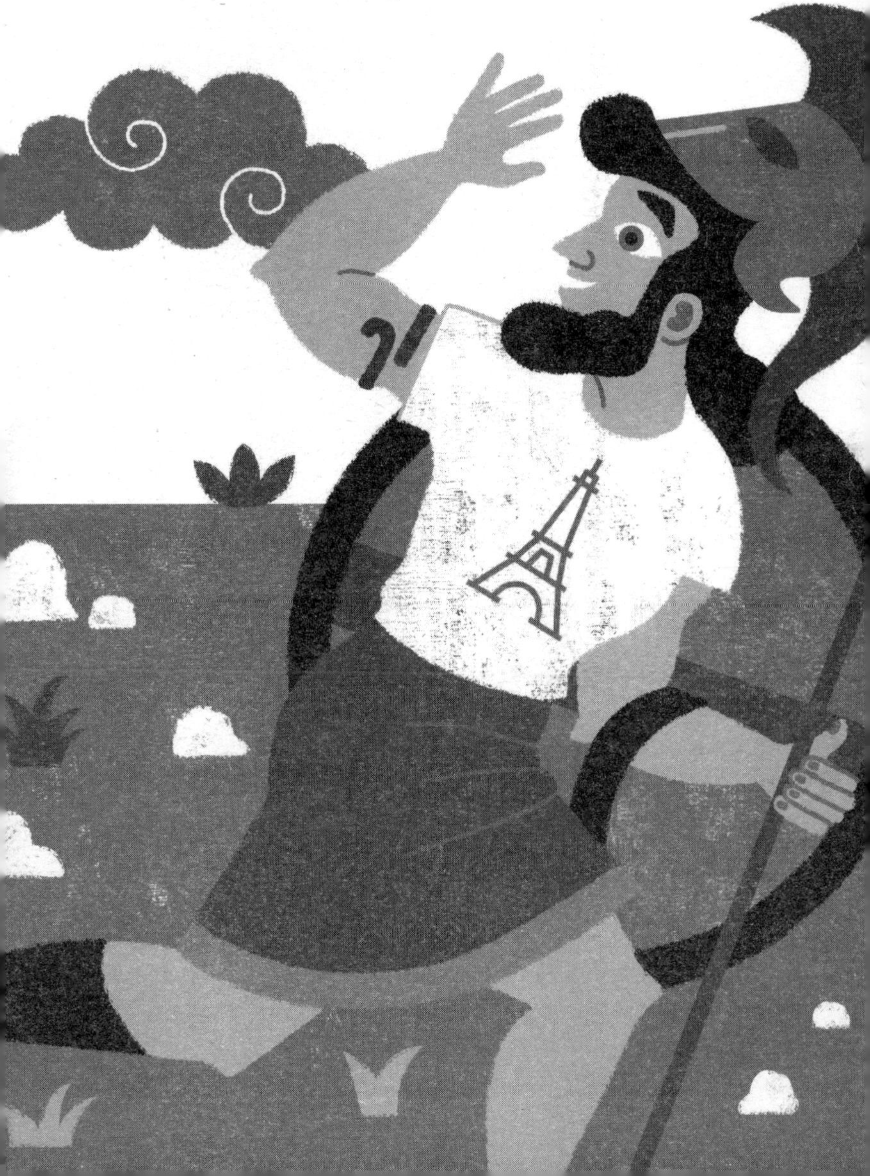

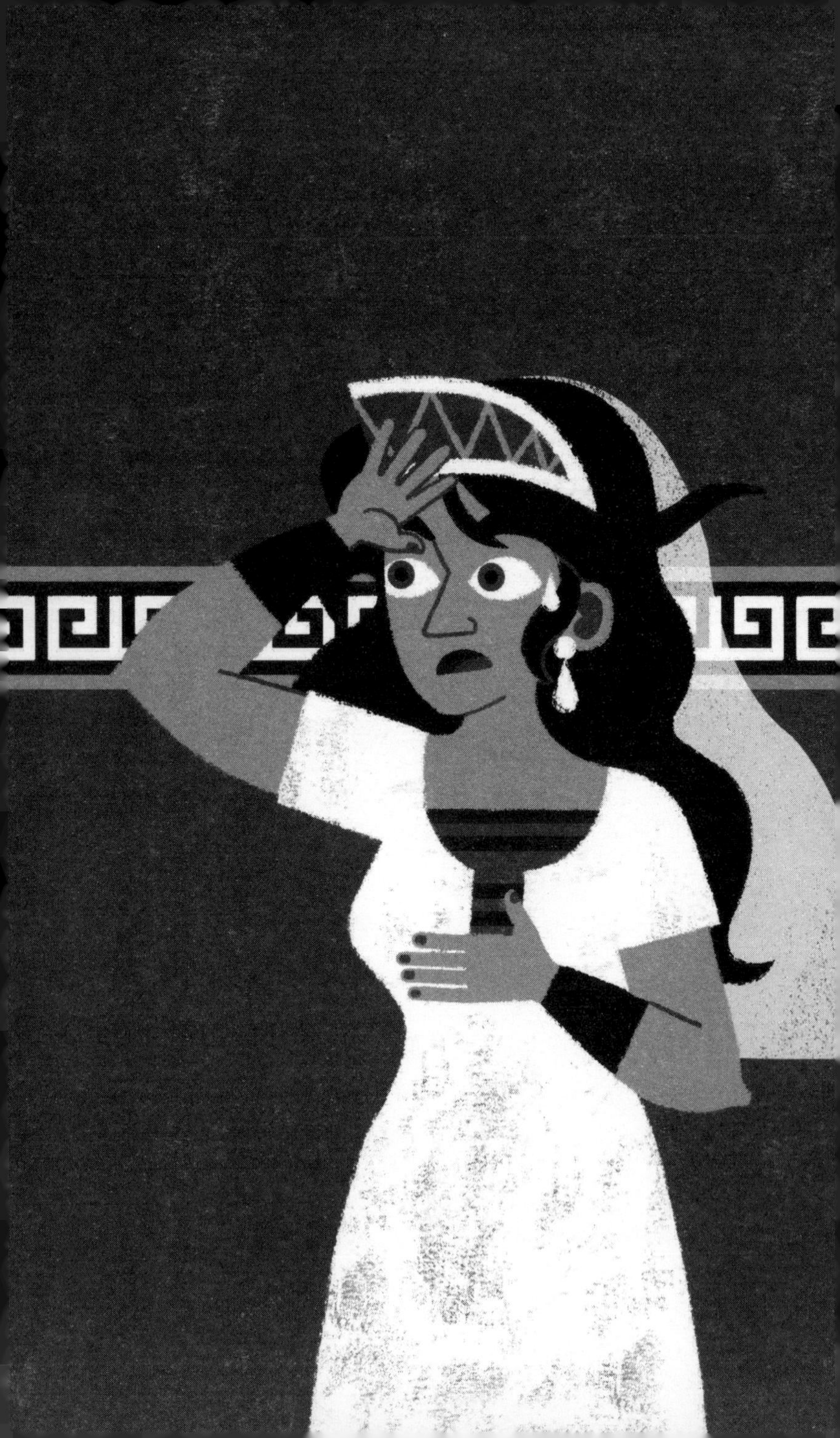

MEANWHILE IN TROY

'We're doomed,' Cassandra says.

'Yes, dear, but I'm busy,' says her brother
Hector, and runs off to wave his willy
at the Greeks.

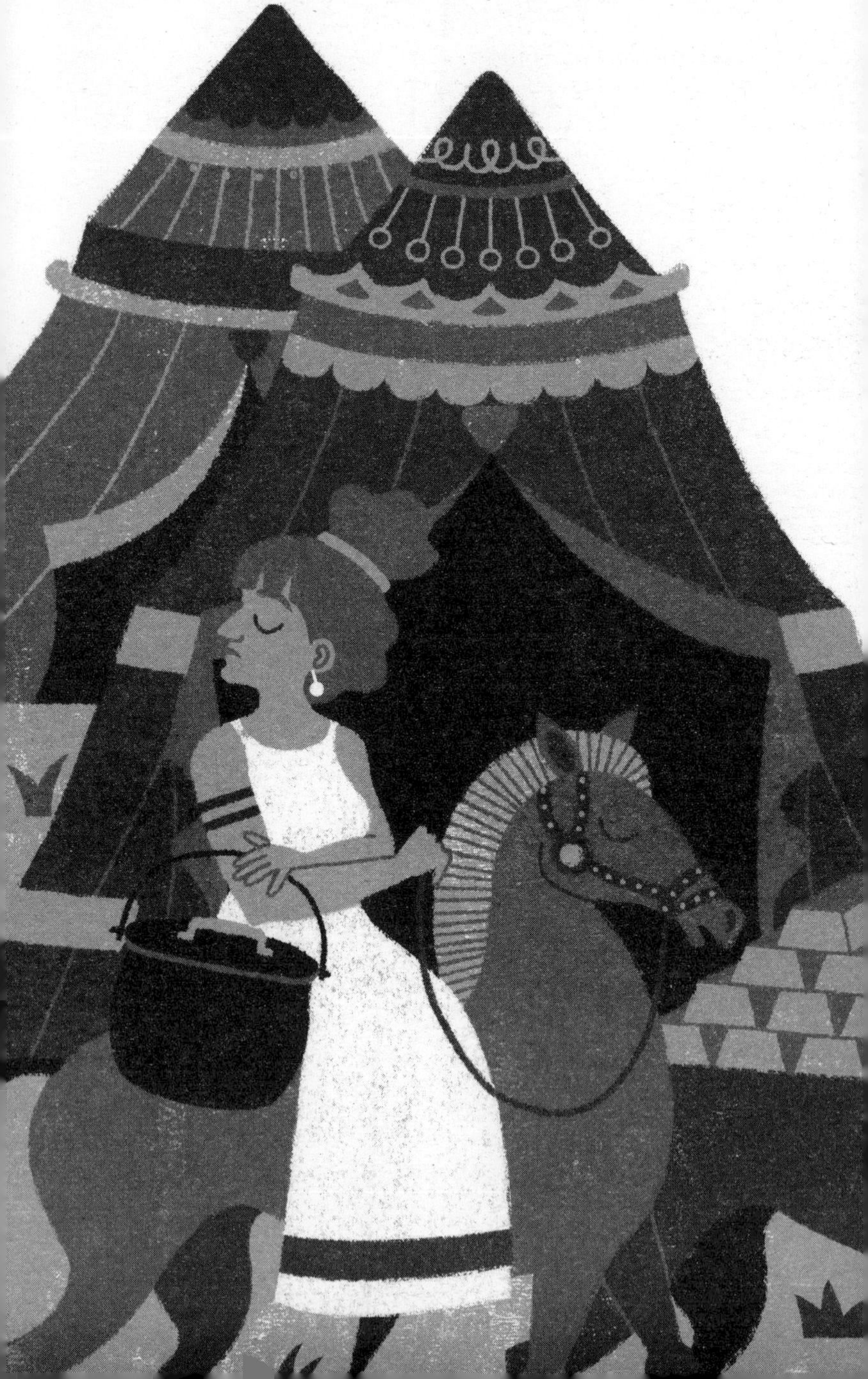

IN THE GREEK CAMP

Agamemnon tries to win back Achilles.
He promises:
Seven tripods
Ten bars of gold
Twenty copper cauldrons
Twelve stallions
Seven women of Lesbos
And Achilles' ex-girlfriend.

As you do.

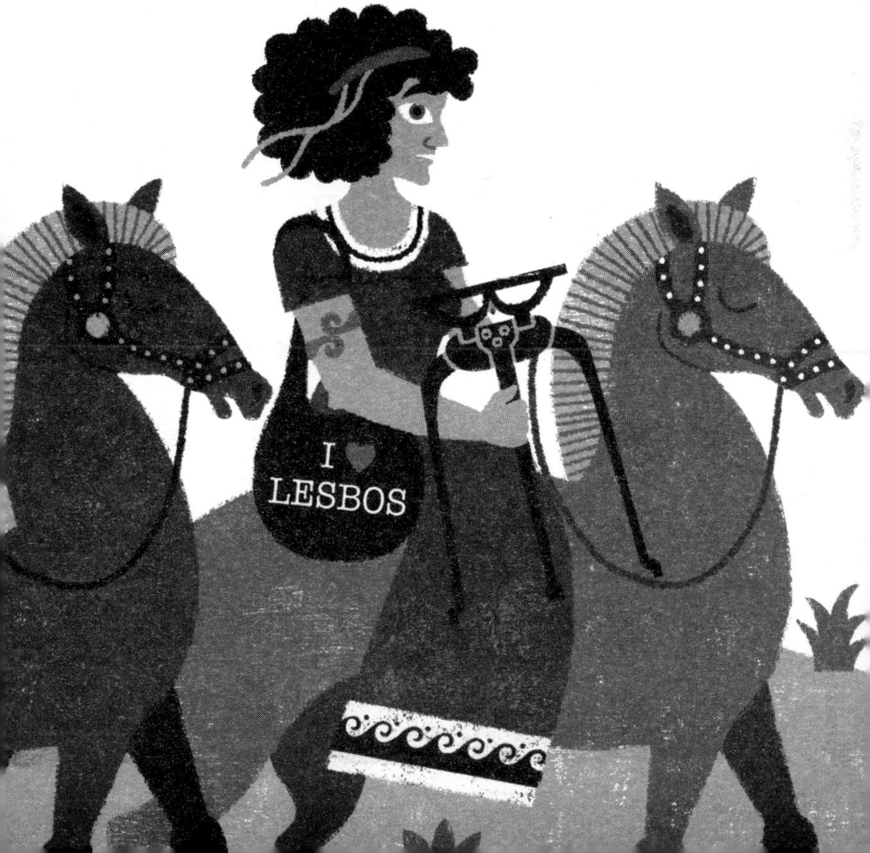
I ♥
LESBOS

ACHILLES IS STILL SULKING

'I haven't slept with her, honest,'
Agamemnon says.

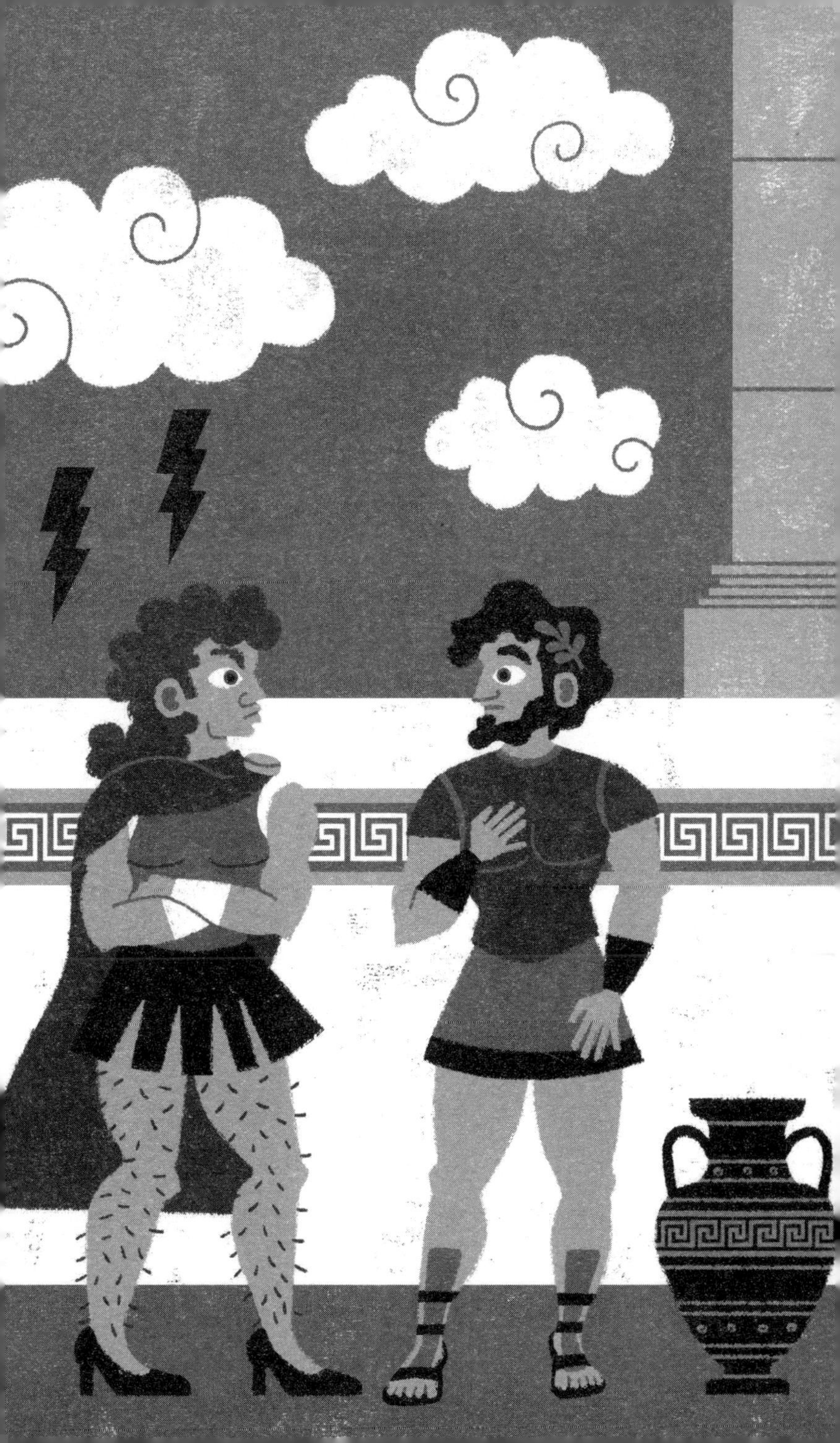

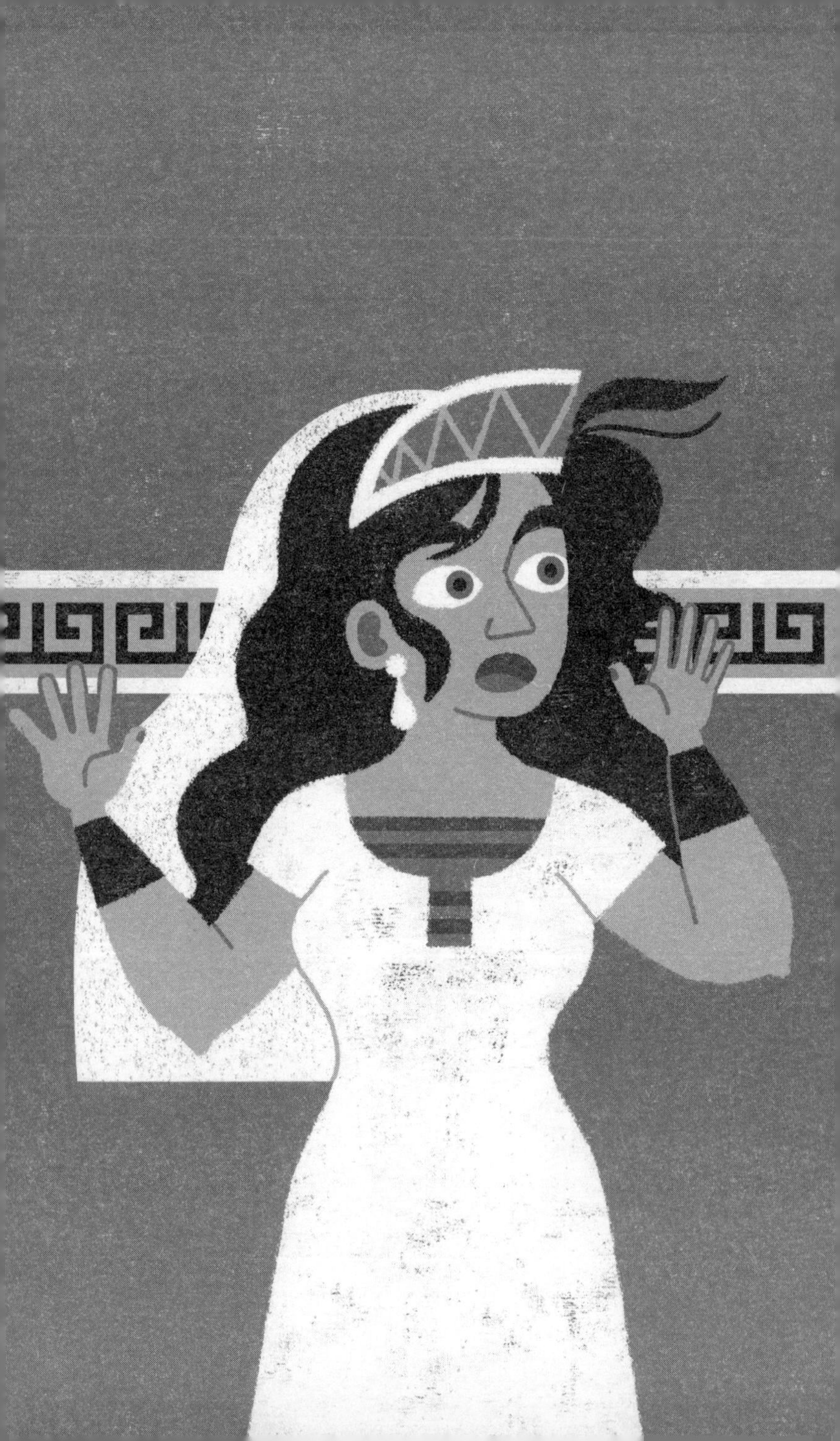

MEANWHILE IN TROY

'Can y'all just stop it with the willy-waving?'
says Helen.

But they can't.

PATROCLUS

Patroclus plays dress-up with Achilles' armour.

Hector shafts him with his mighty spear.

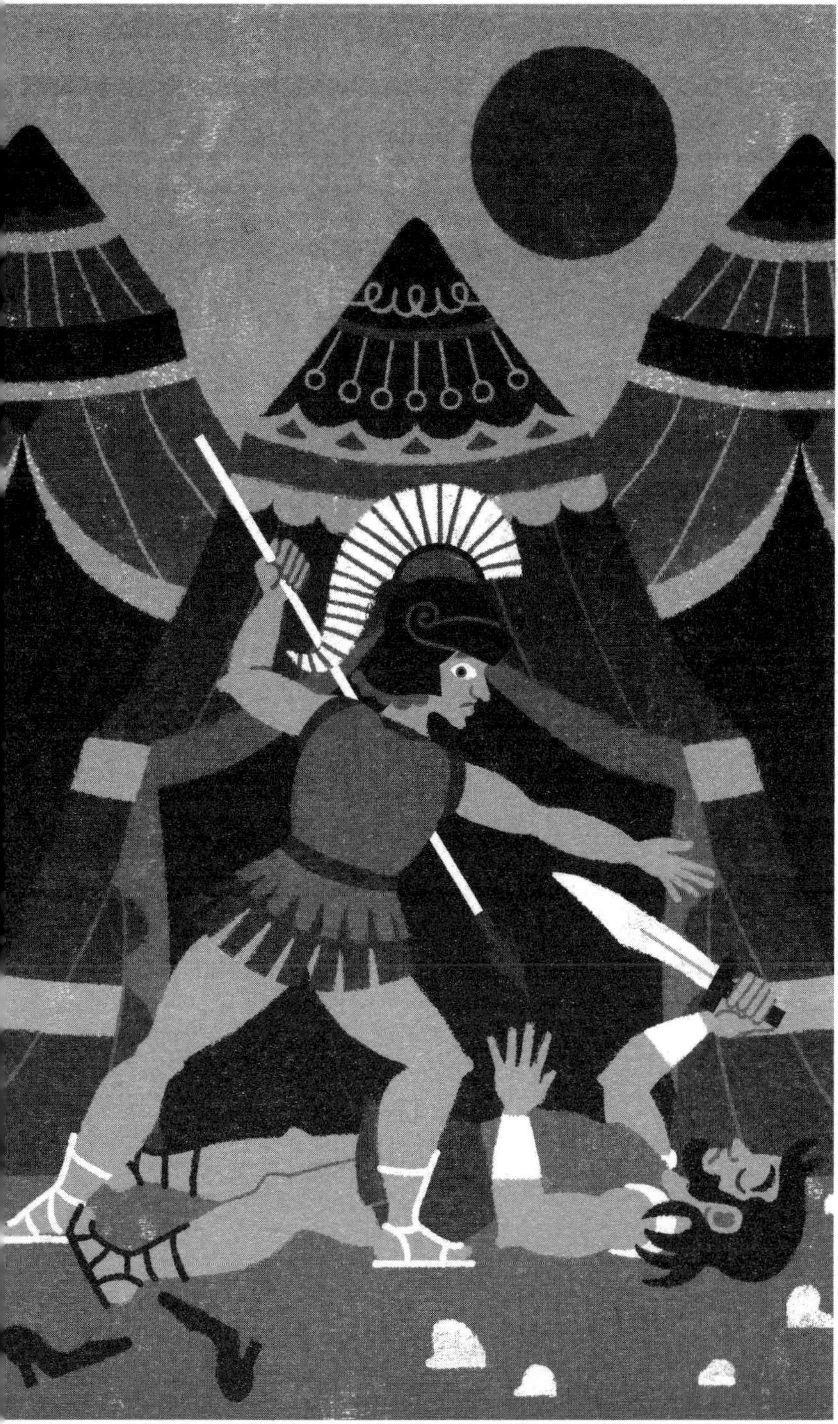

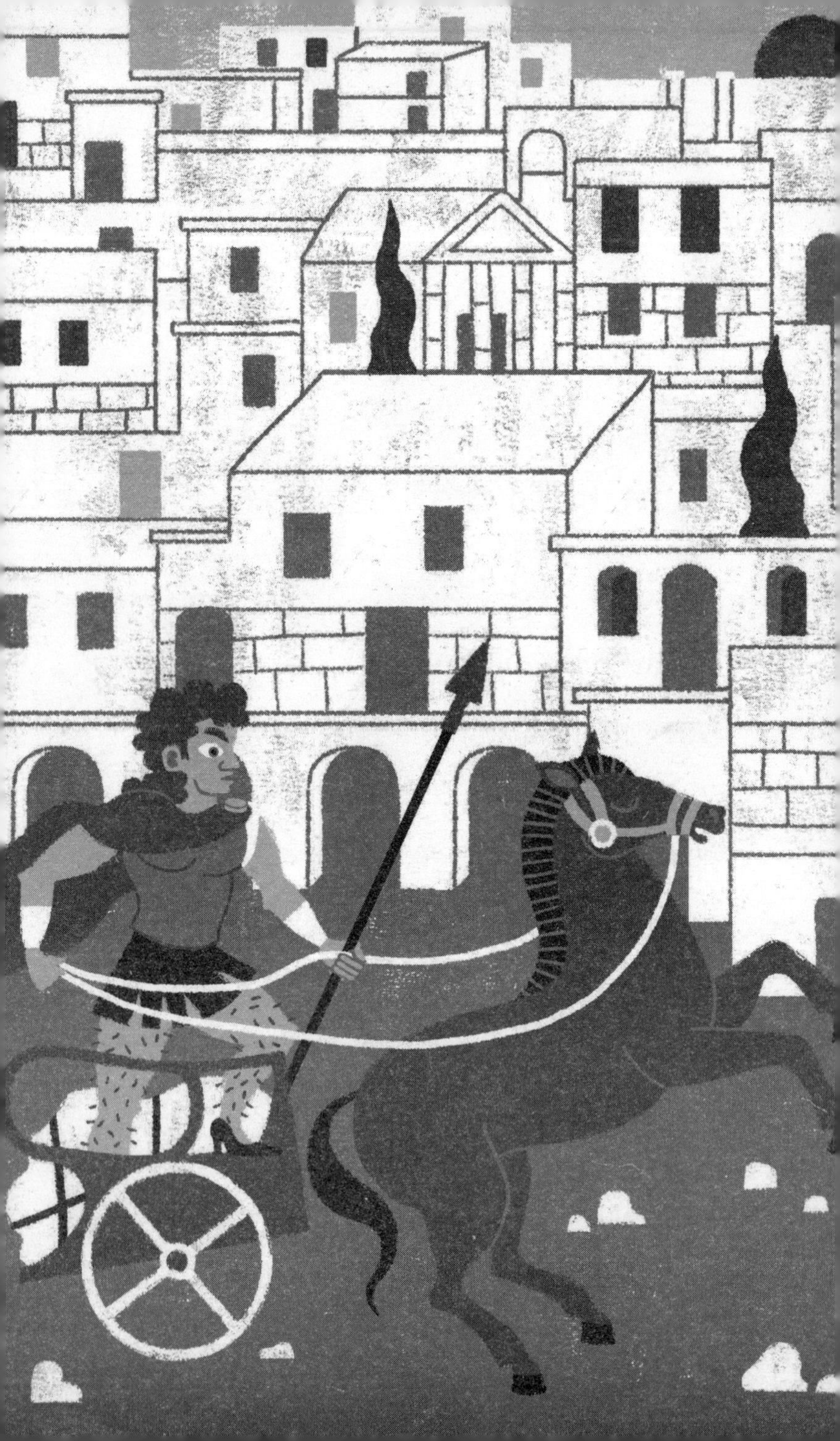

ACHILLES REJOINS THE FIGHT

When Patroclus dies, Achilles stops sulking.

After all, he also has a mighty spear!

He kills Hector, then straps the corpse to his chariot and runs rings around Troy.

An early attempt to doughnut.

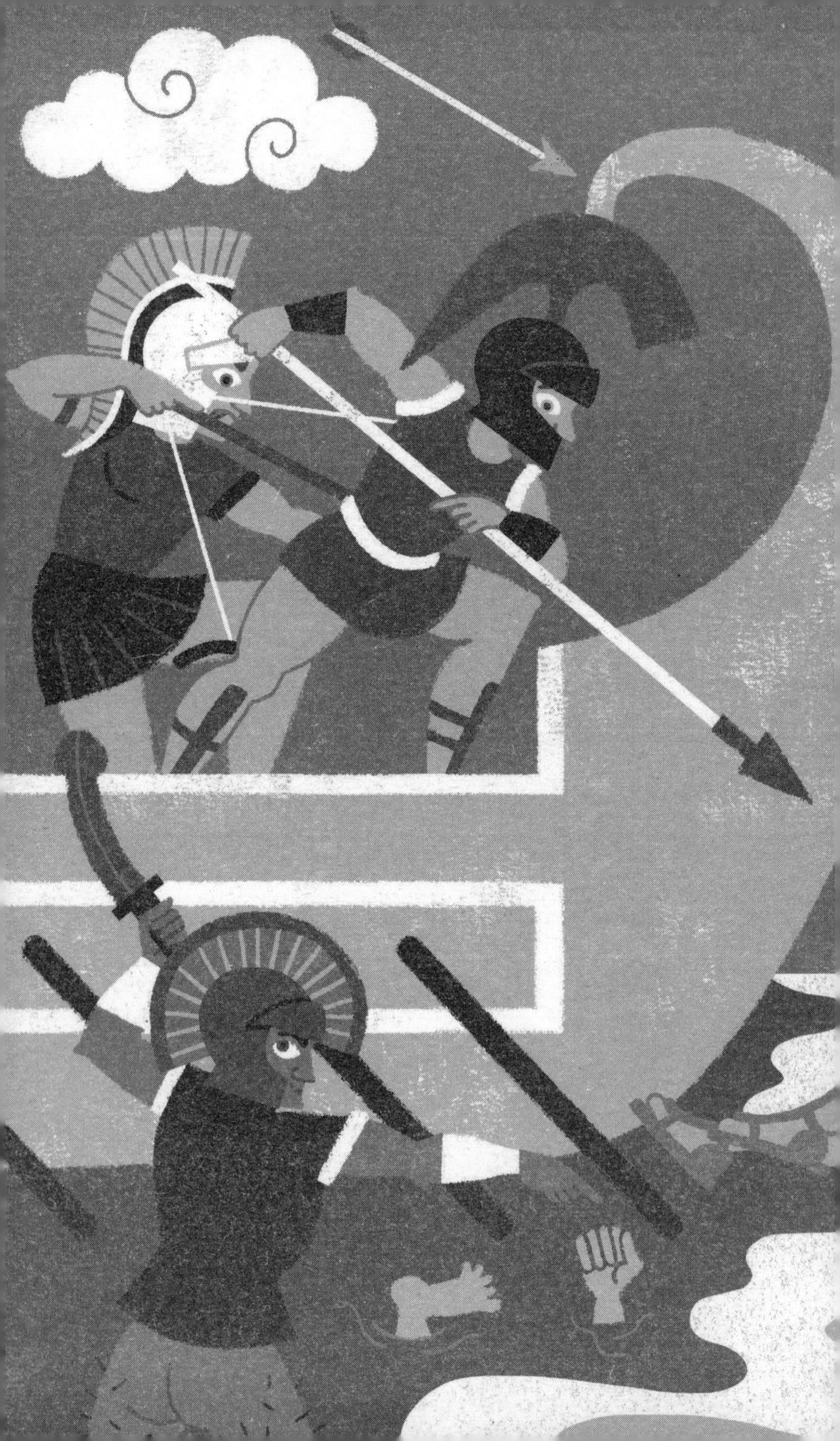

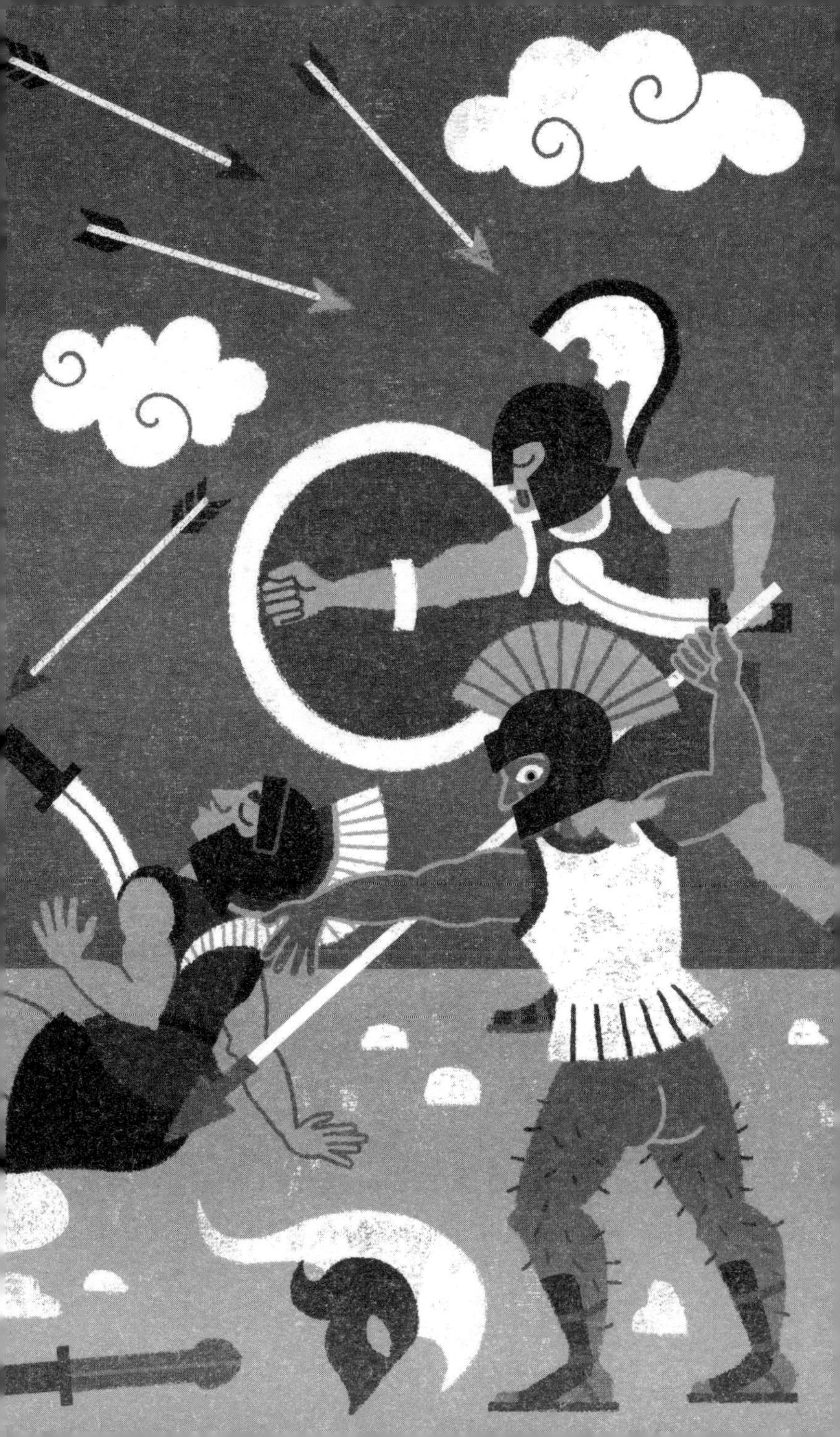

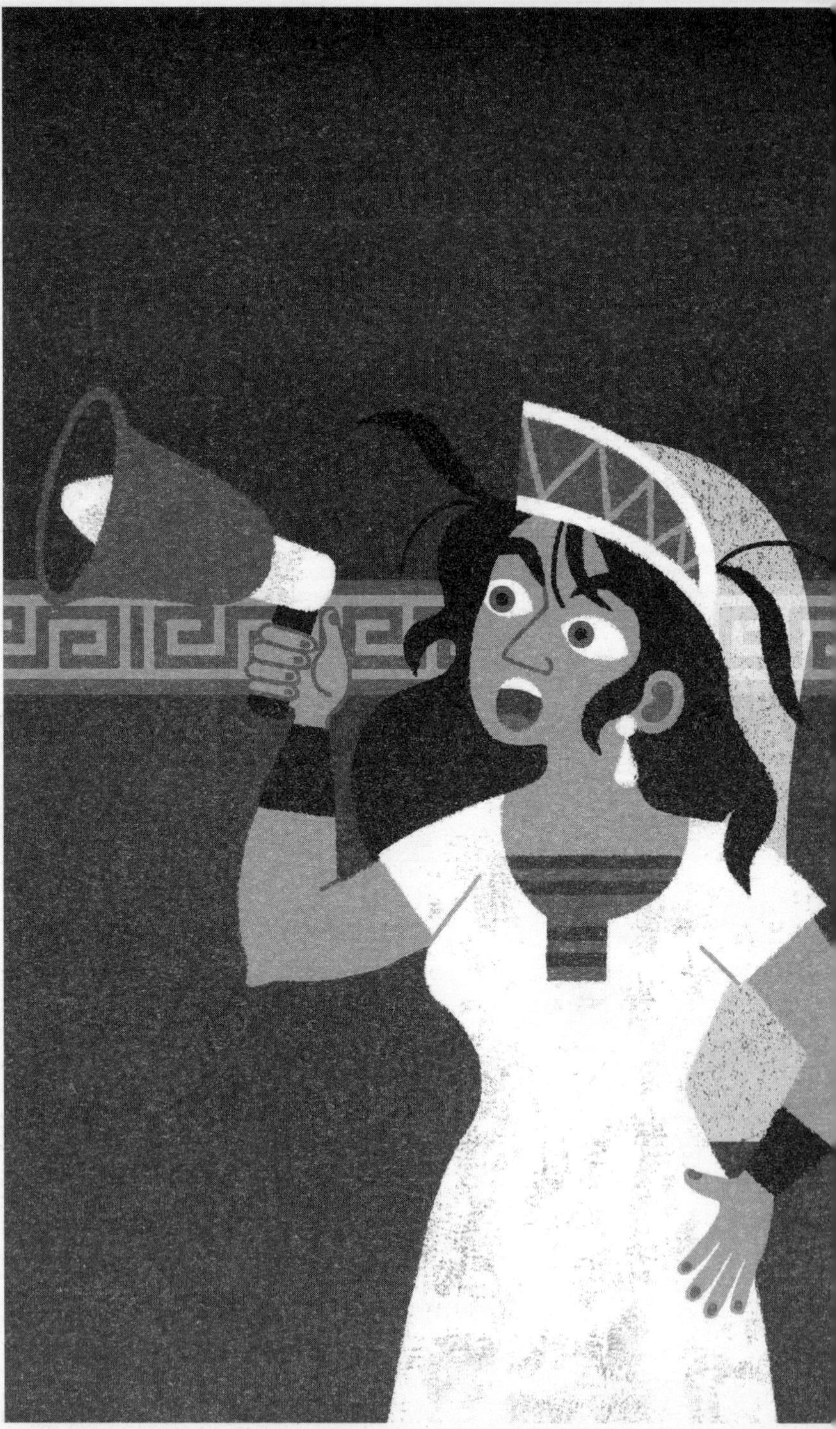

MEANWHILE IN TROY

'We're all going to die,' says Cassandra,
to no one in particular.

It's not as if anyone was listening anyway.

ACHILLES

In the end, it all gets too much. His heels
are killing him.

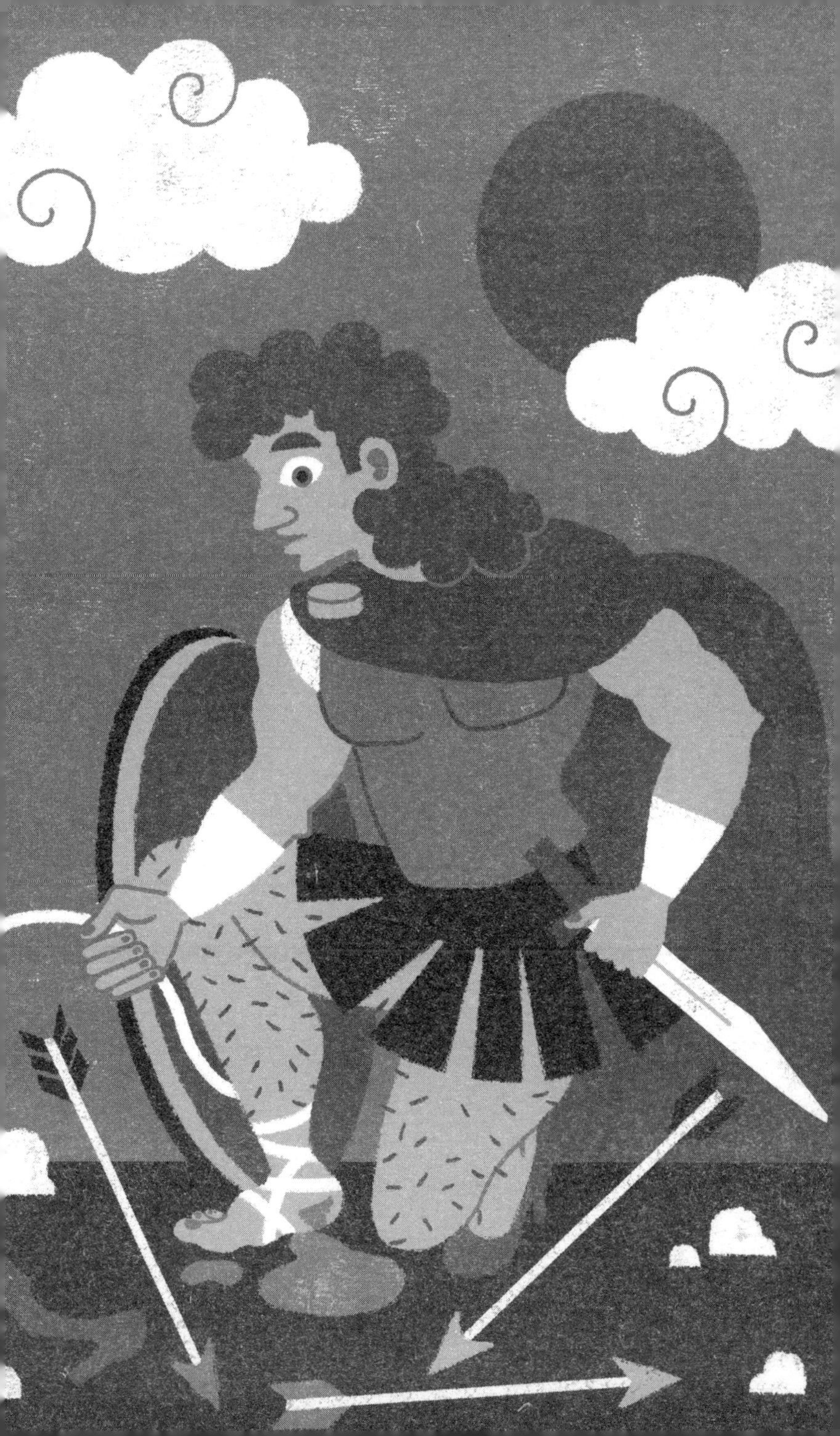

BIG AJAX FIGHTS FOR ACHILLES' ARMOUR

Big Ajax wants the dead man's armour.

Odysseus tells Big Ajax to put it away.

Big Ajax doesn't.

So, he dies.

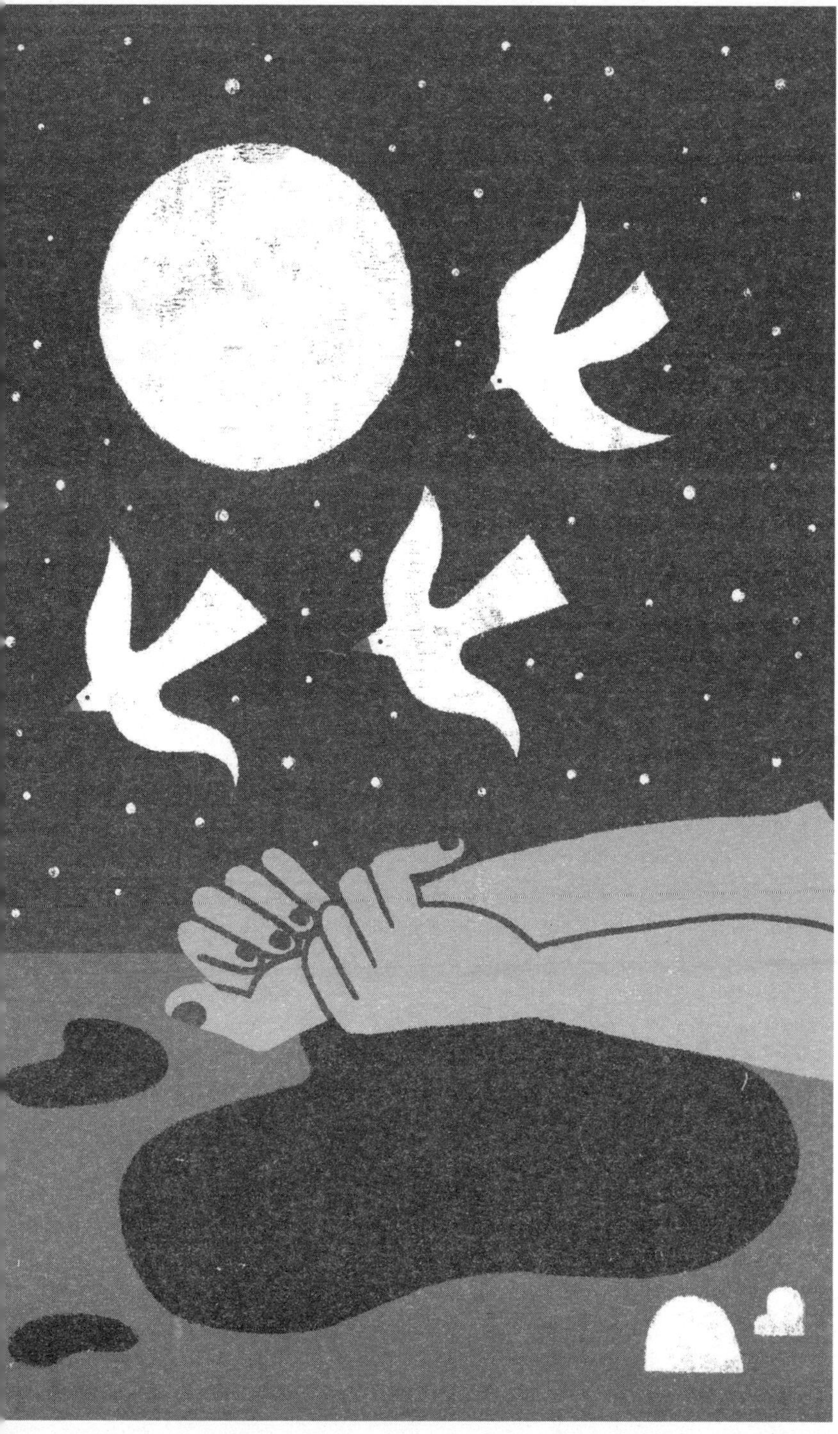

CASSANDRA

'Don't open the gates! Don't take in the horse!' Cassandra cries.

They open the gates.

They take in the horse.

They all die.

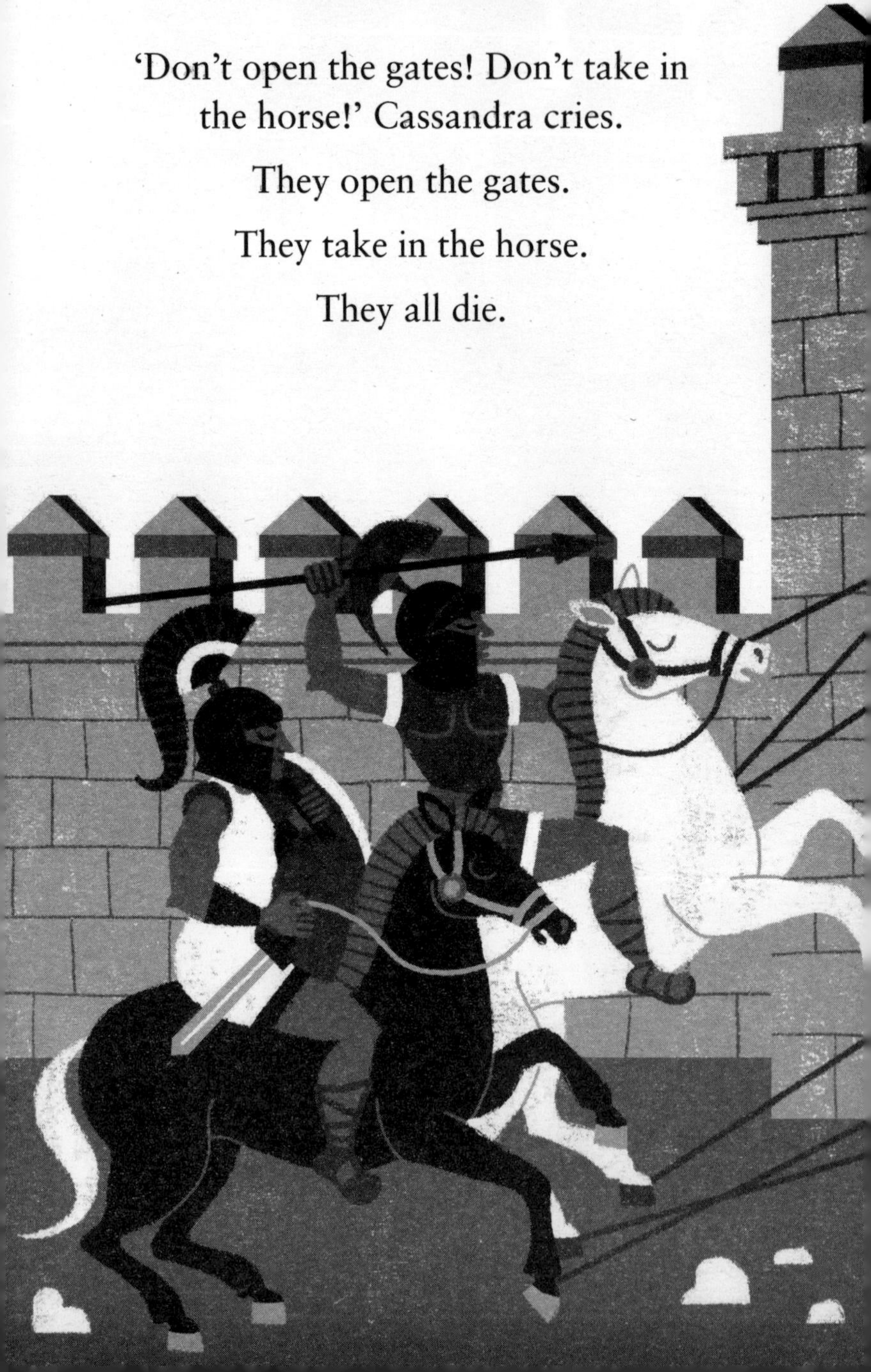

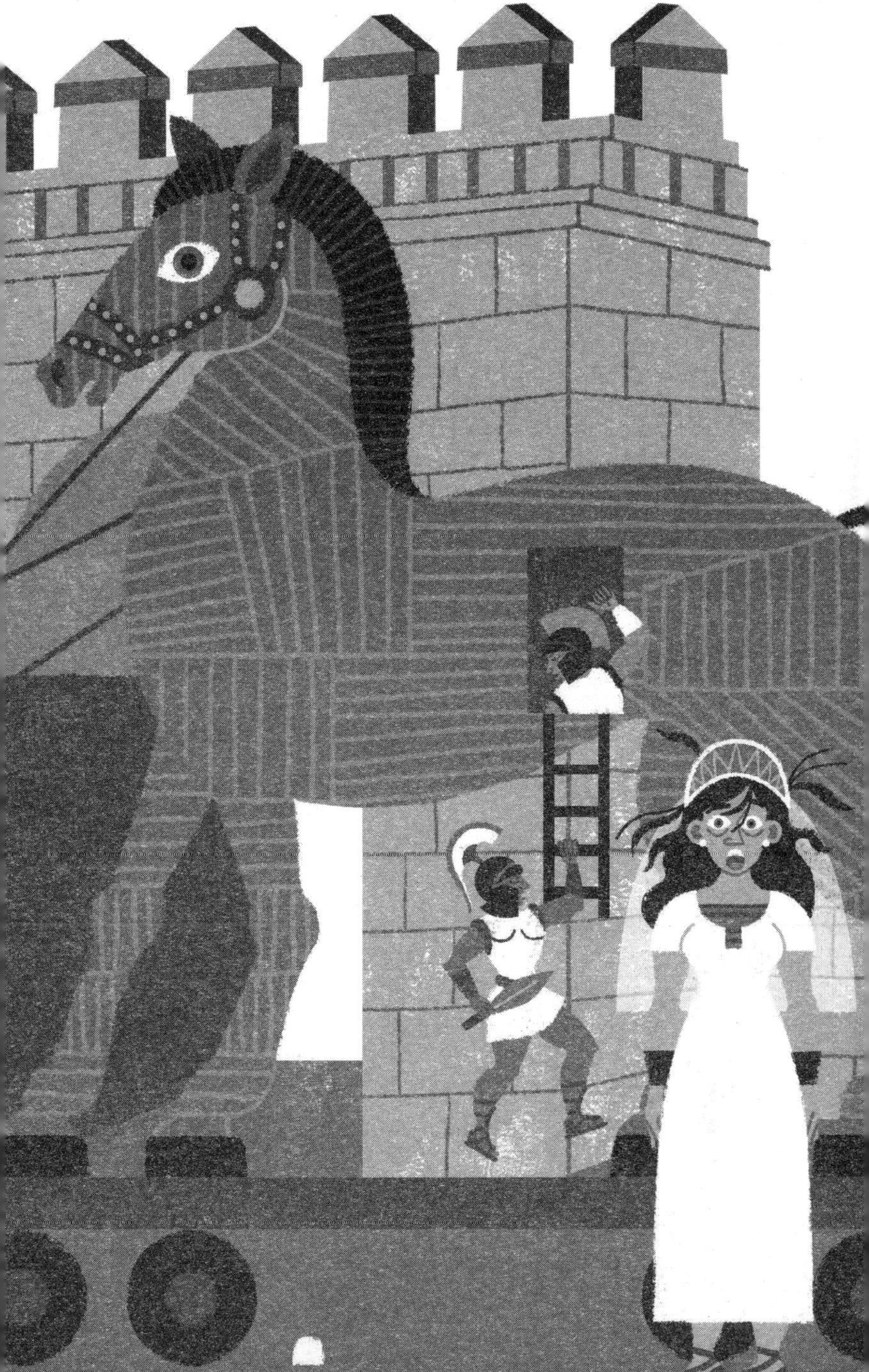

The
Odyssey

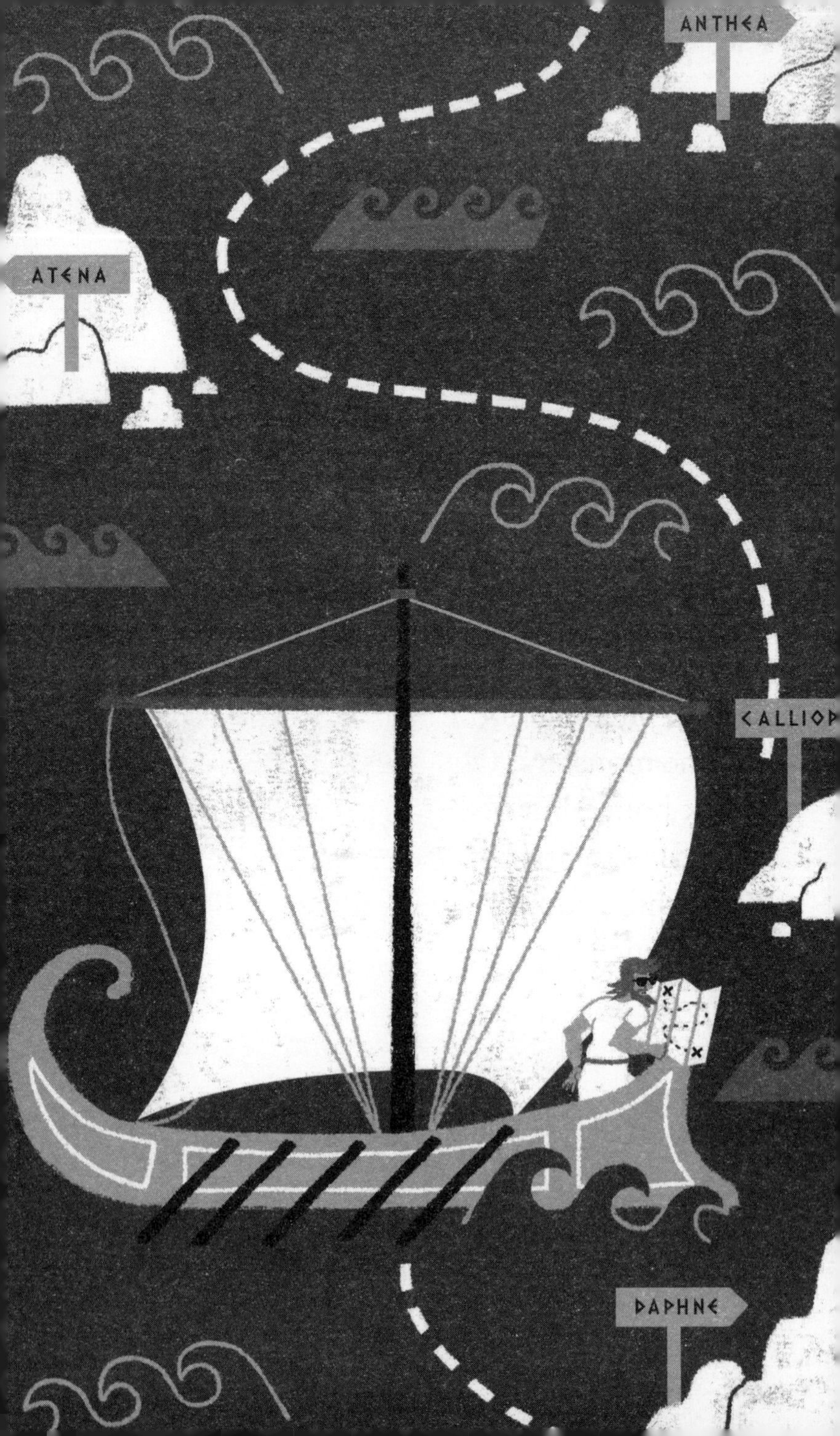
ANTHEA
ATENA
CALLIOP
DAPHNE

TLDR: The Odyssey – A Long Story Involving Lots of Sex

After raping and looting in Troy and slaying some monsters, Odysseus is ready to go back home, but he keeps getting stuck on islands with attractive women, poor thing. Meanwhile, back home on Ithaca, Odysseus' wife Penelope is a single mum for twenty years.

WHO'S WHO: THE ODYSSEY

ODYSSEUS

King of Ithaca, husband of Penelope

Greek hero. Pretty rubbish at map reading.

PENELOPE

Queen of Ithaca, wife of Odysseus

Waits twenty years for her husband to learn how to read
a map and sail a boat.

ITHACA

Home island of Odysseus and Penelope.

CIRCE

Single sorceress living her best life
on a Mediterranean island.

NYMPH CALYPSO

Nymph living her best life on another Mediterranean island.

THE SIRENS

Mermaids living their best life on a rock.

THE SUITORS

Everyone thinks that Odysseus is dead, and Penelope cannot possibly live without a man in her life. So, a bunch of chancers land in Ithaca to vie for Penelope's hand.

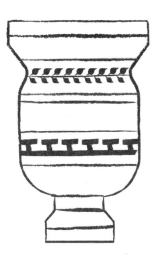

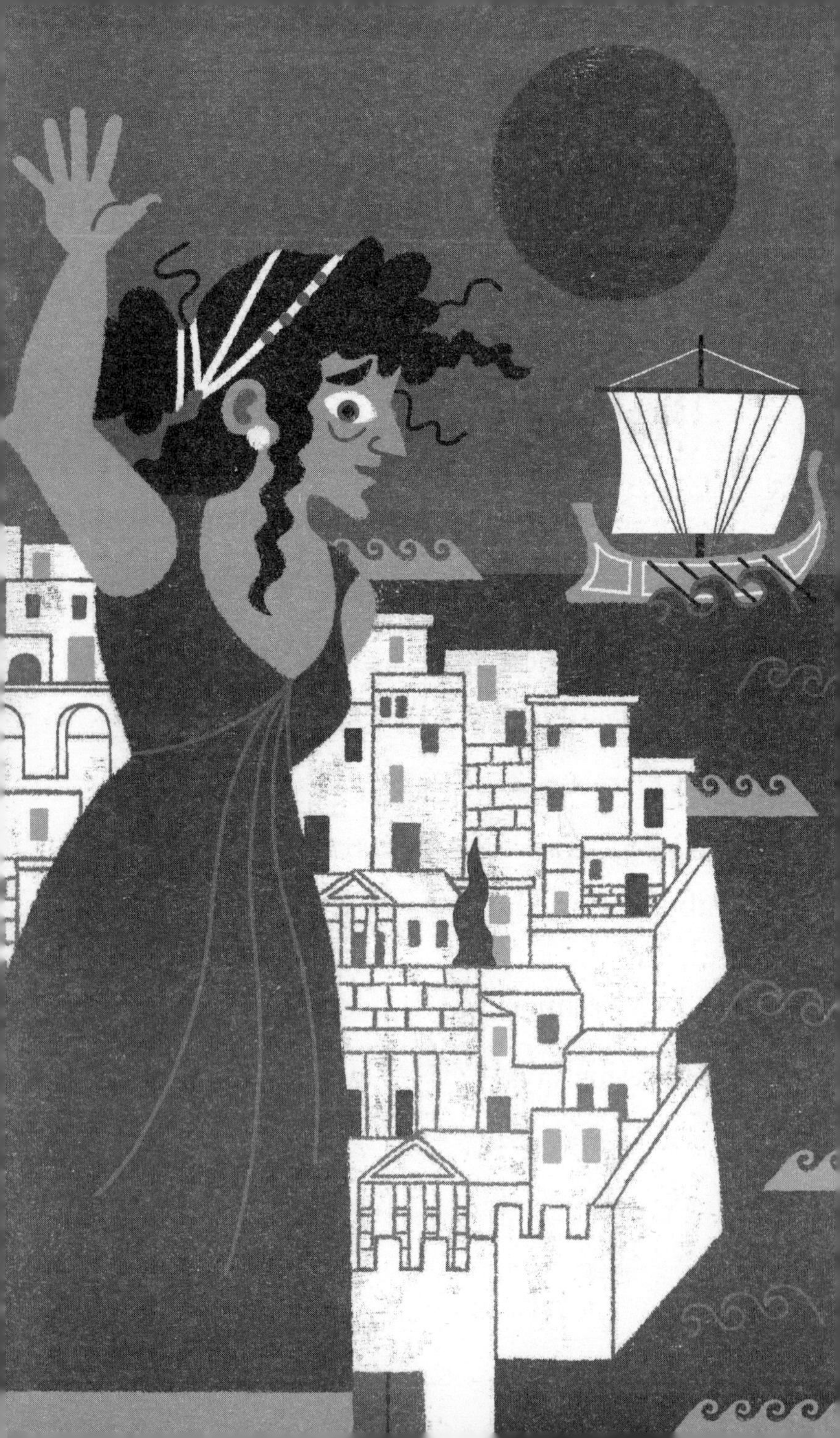

ODYSSEUS LEAVES
ITHACA FOR TROY

Odysseus says he's going cruising with the lads.

Penelope says that's fine. She'll look after the baby. And the house. And the goats. And the island. And the kingdom.

Odysseus says he'll be back later.

Penelope says that when she isn't looking after the baby, and the house, and the goats, and the island, and the kingdom, maybe she might try to finish some weaving.

Odysseus says, 'OK, honeybun, bye,' and leaves.

ODYSSEUS INVENTS THE TROJAN HORSE

It only takes Odysseus ten years to come up with the idea of the wooden horse. He is very proud of it.

Now the war is over, he wants to sail home but, distracted by thoughts of his own genius, he keeps losing his way.

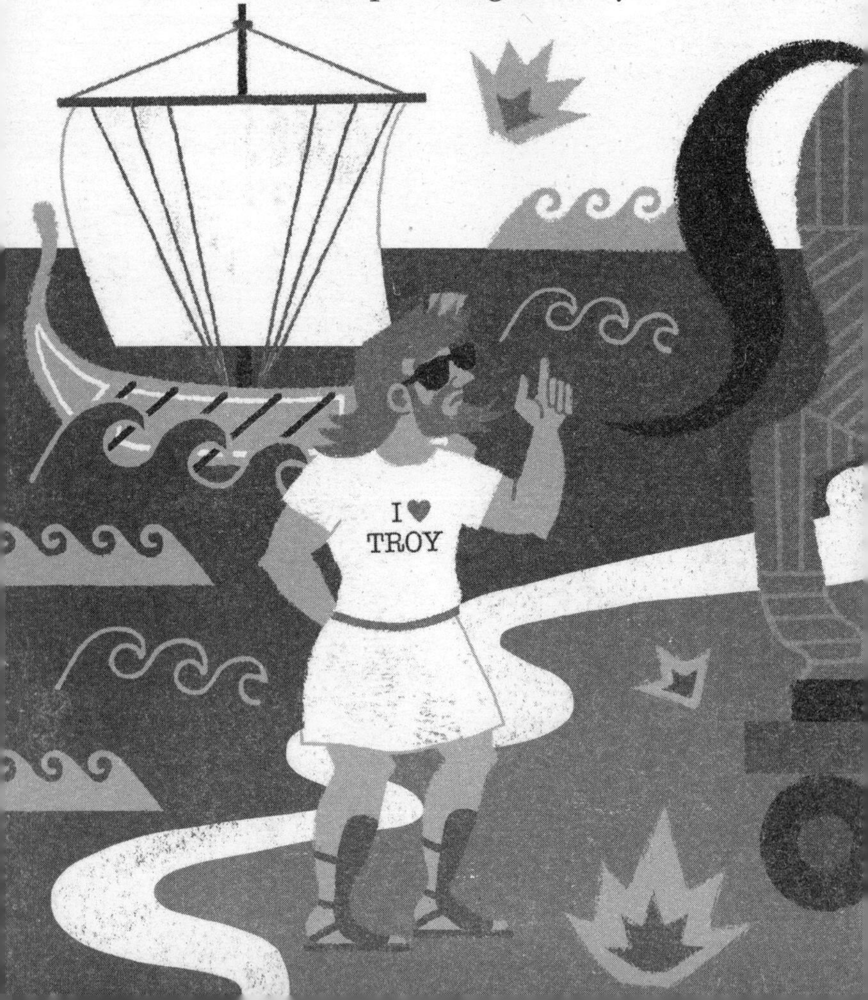
I ♥
TROY

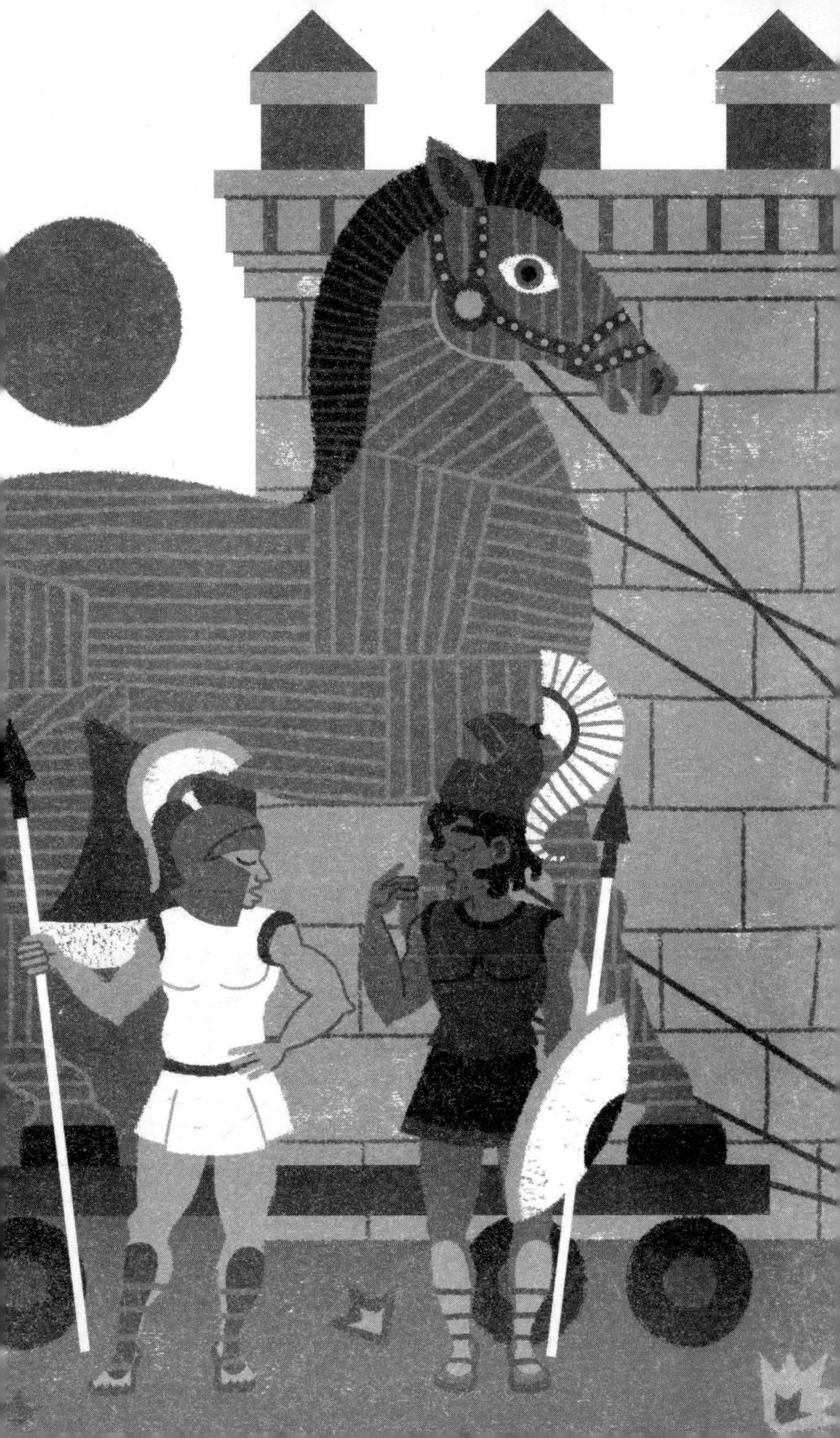

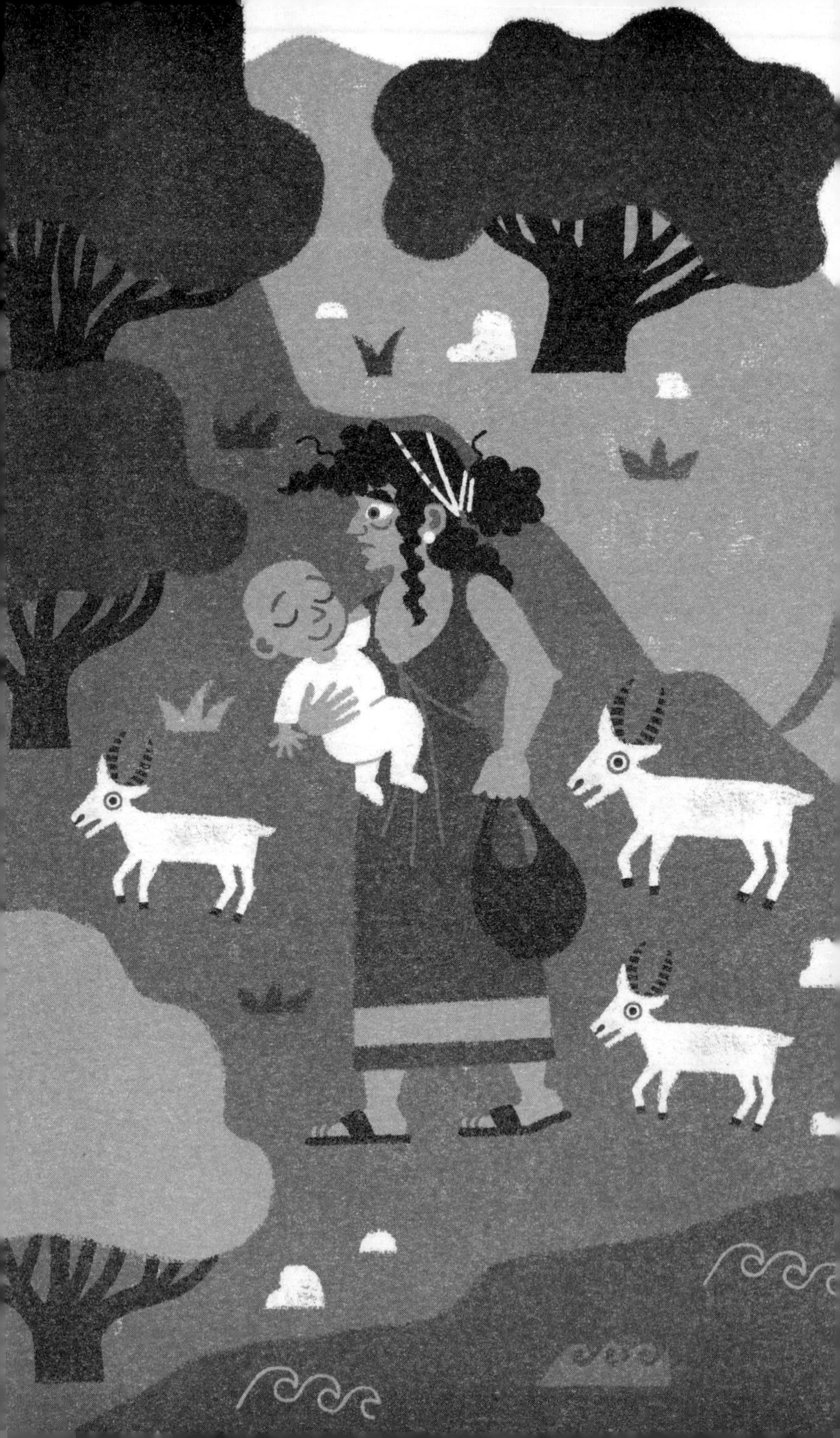

MEANWHILE ON ITHACA

Penelope is looking after the child, and the house, and the goats, and the island, and the kingdom.

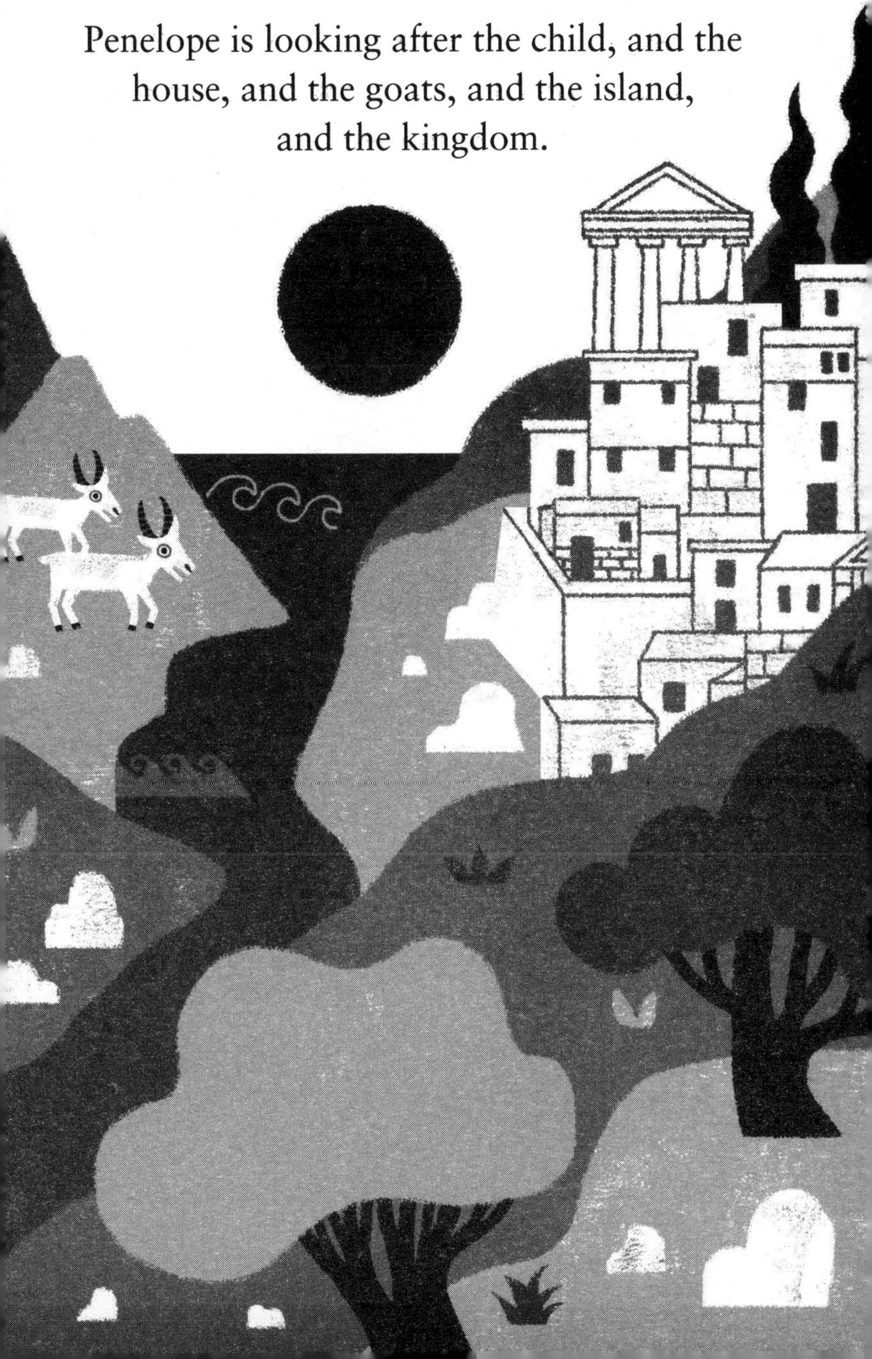

ODYSSEUS GETS STUCK ON POWERFUL SORCERESS CIRCE'S ISLAND

Odysseus shows her his sword.

Circe swoons and gives up her powers.

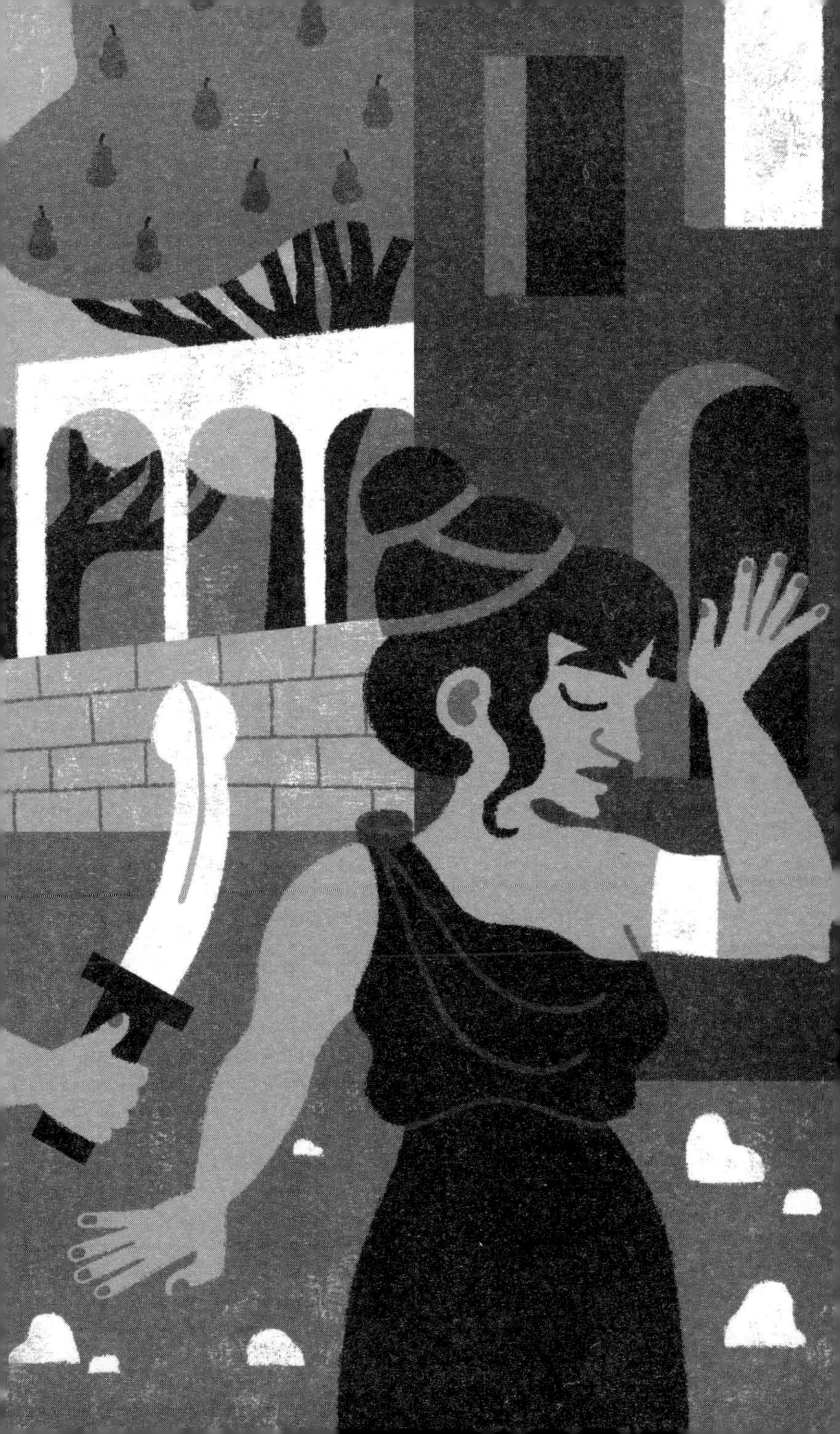

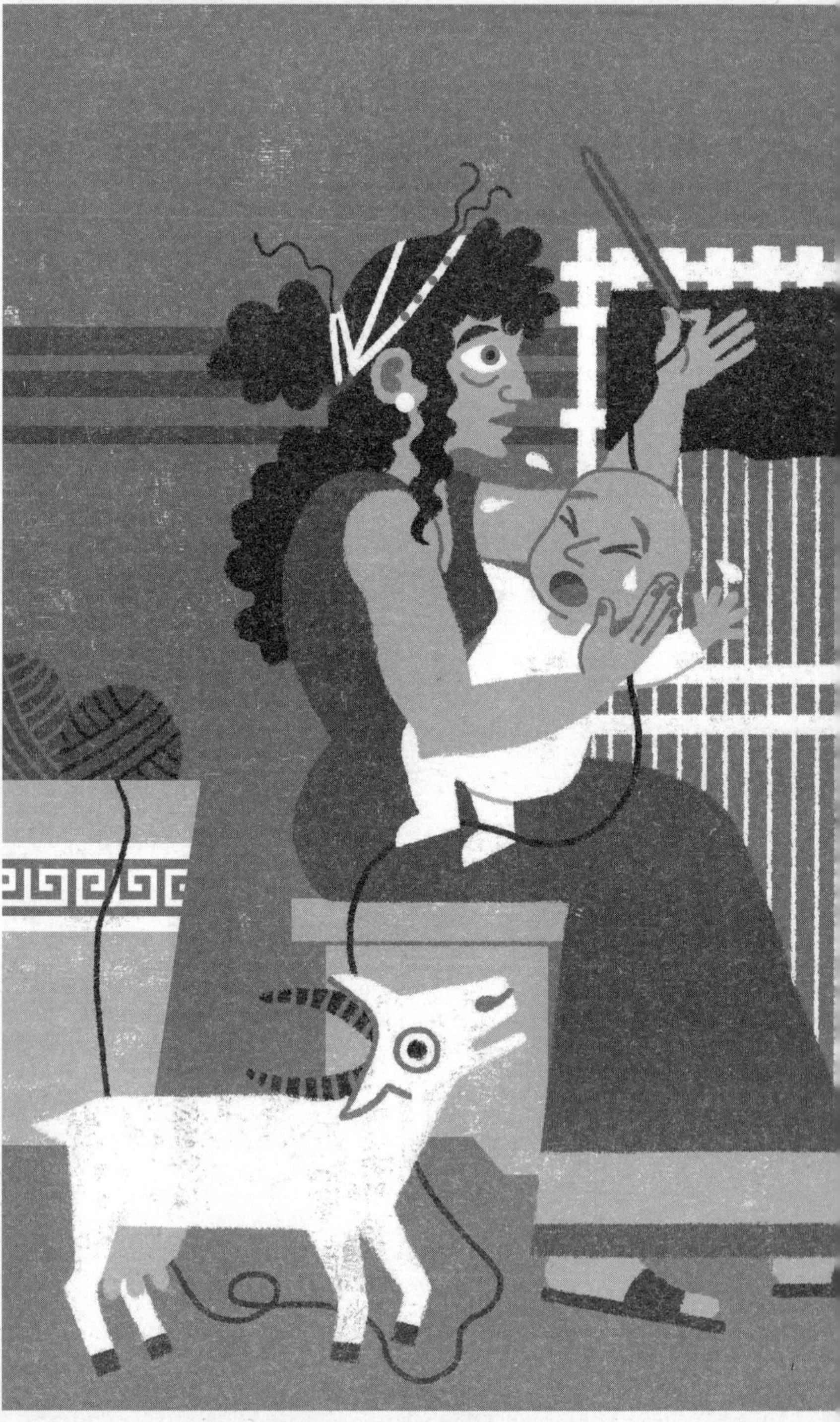

MEANWHILE ON ITHACA

Penelope doesn't have much time for weaving.

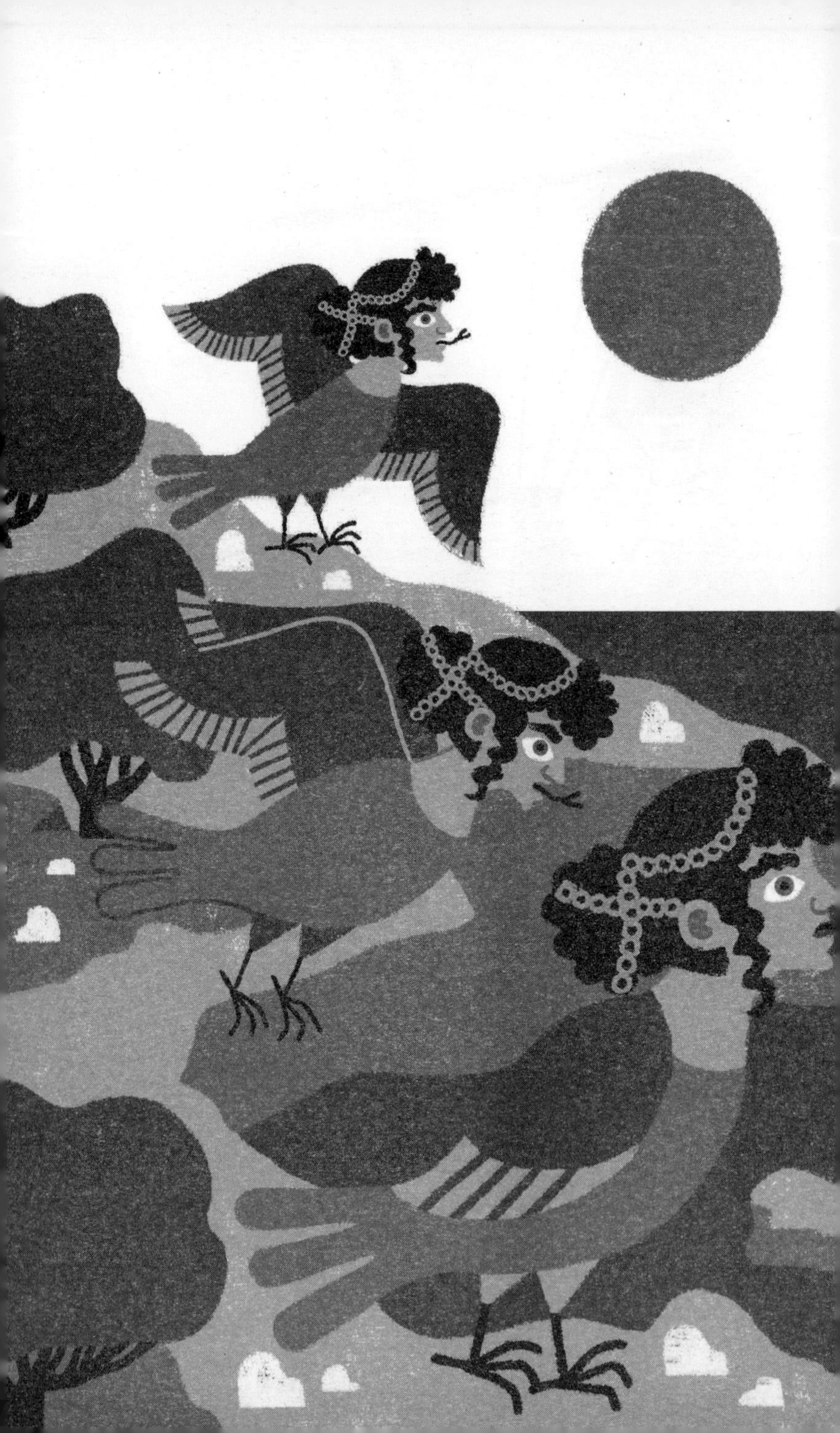

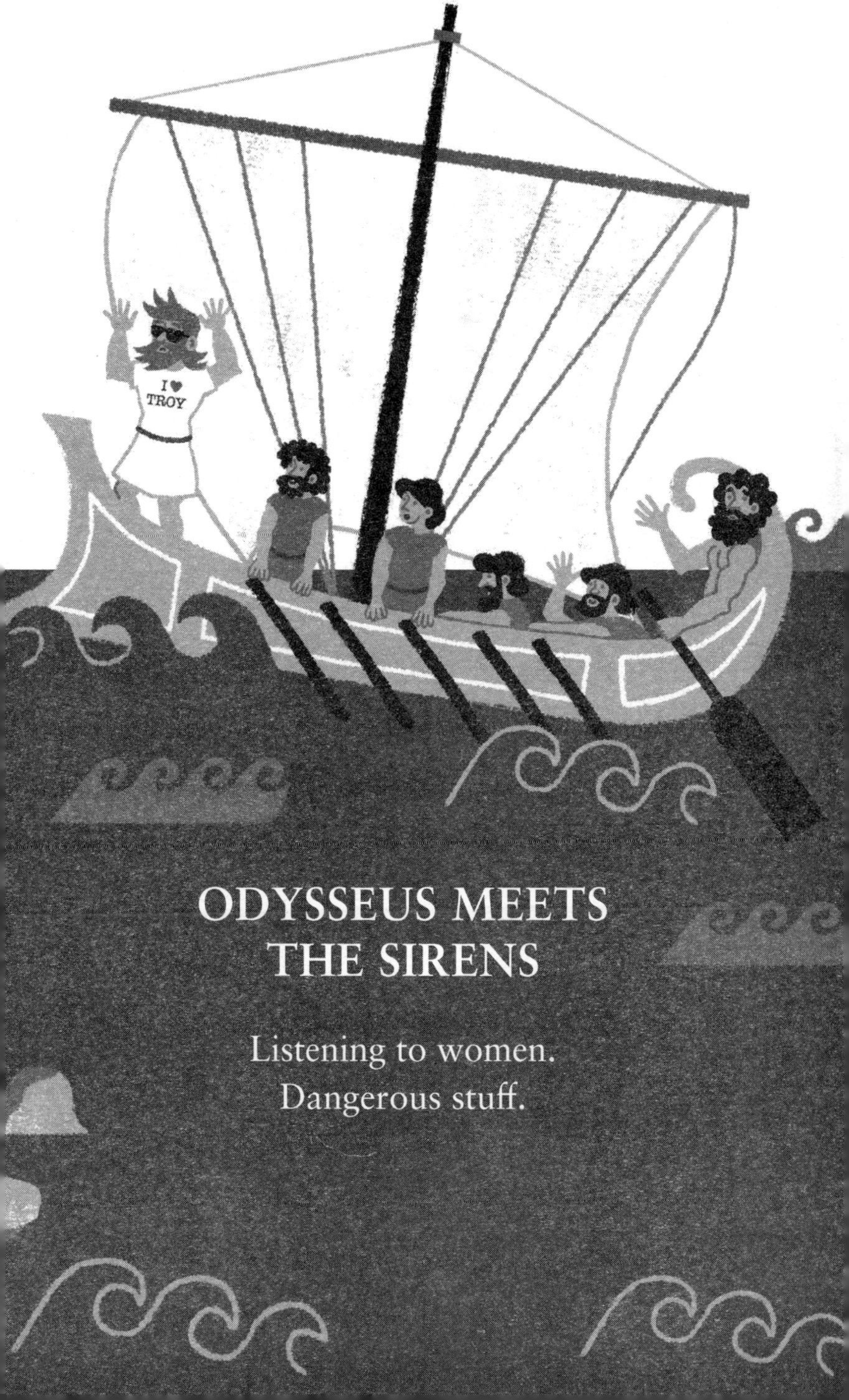
I ♥
TROY

ODYSSEUS MEETS THE SIRENS

Listening to women.
Dangerous stuff.

MEANWHILE ON ITHACA

The suitors aren't helping with the teenager,
or the house, or the goats, or the island,
or the kingdom.

Let alone the weaving.

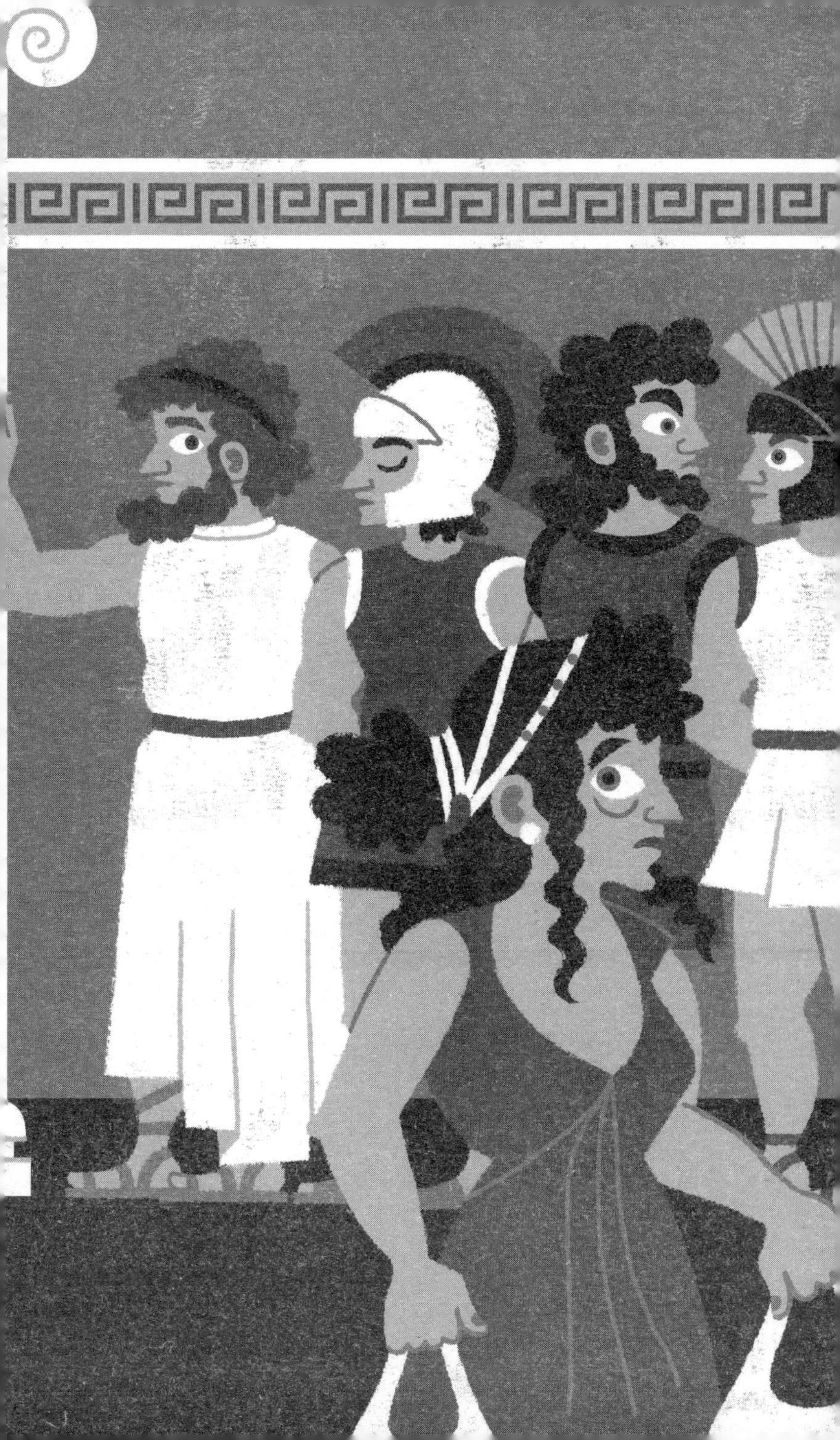

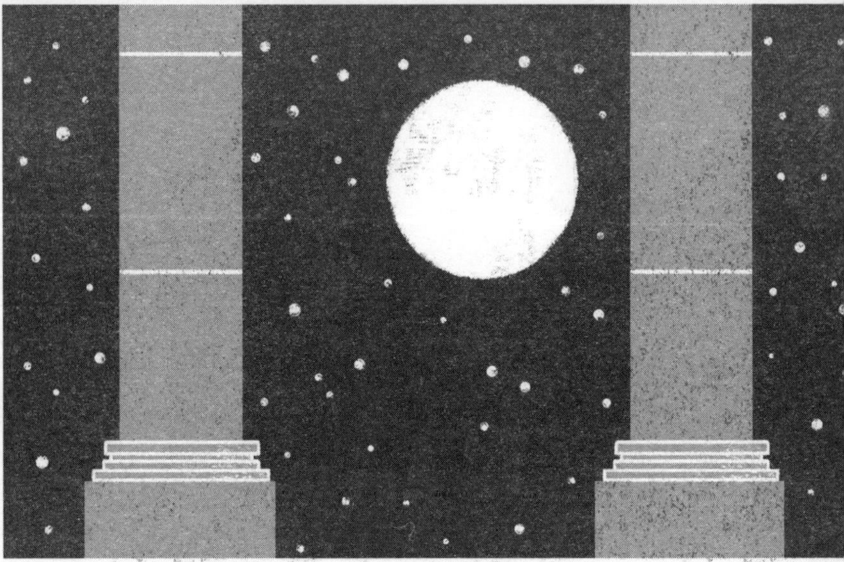

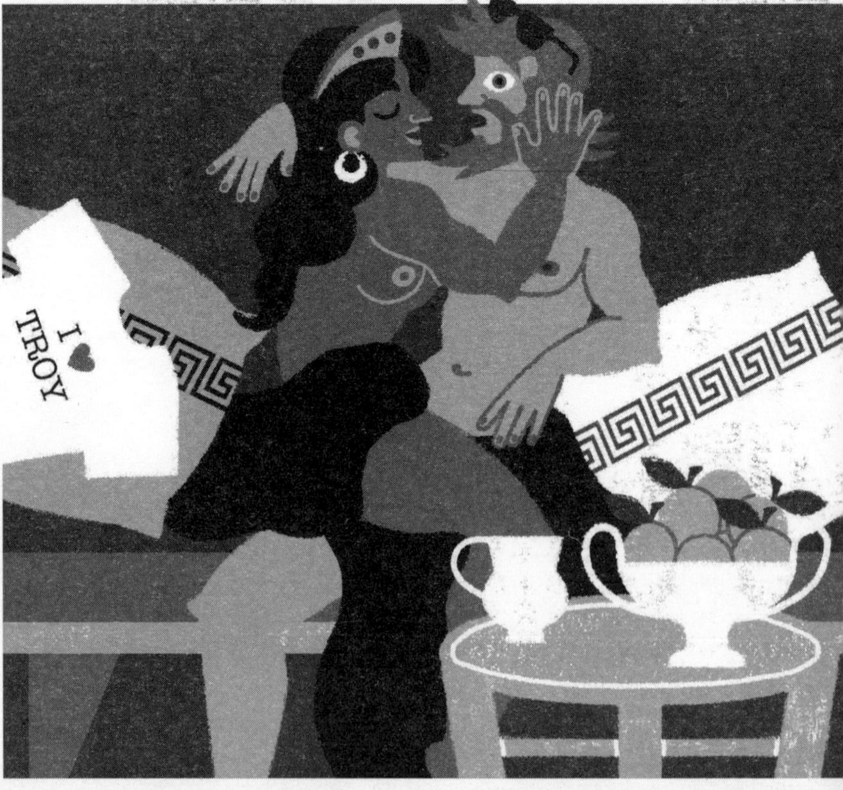
I ♥ TROY

ODYSSEUS IS HELD CAPTIVE BY THE NYMPH CALYPSO

'Strange. It's usually me on top,'
Odysseus says.

ODYSSEUS RETURNS TO ITHACA

The suitors have raped the maids of Ithaca.

So, Odysseus first kills the suitors,
then murders the maids.

Collateral damage.

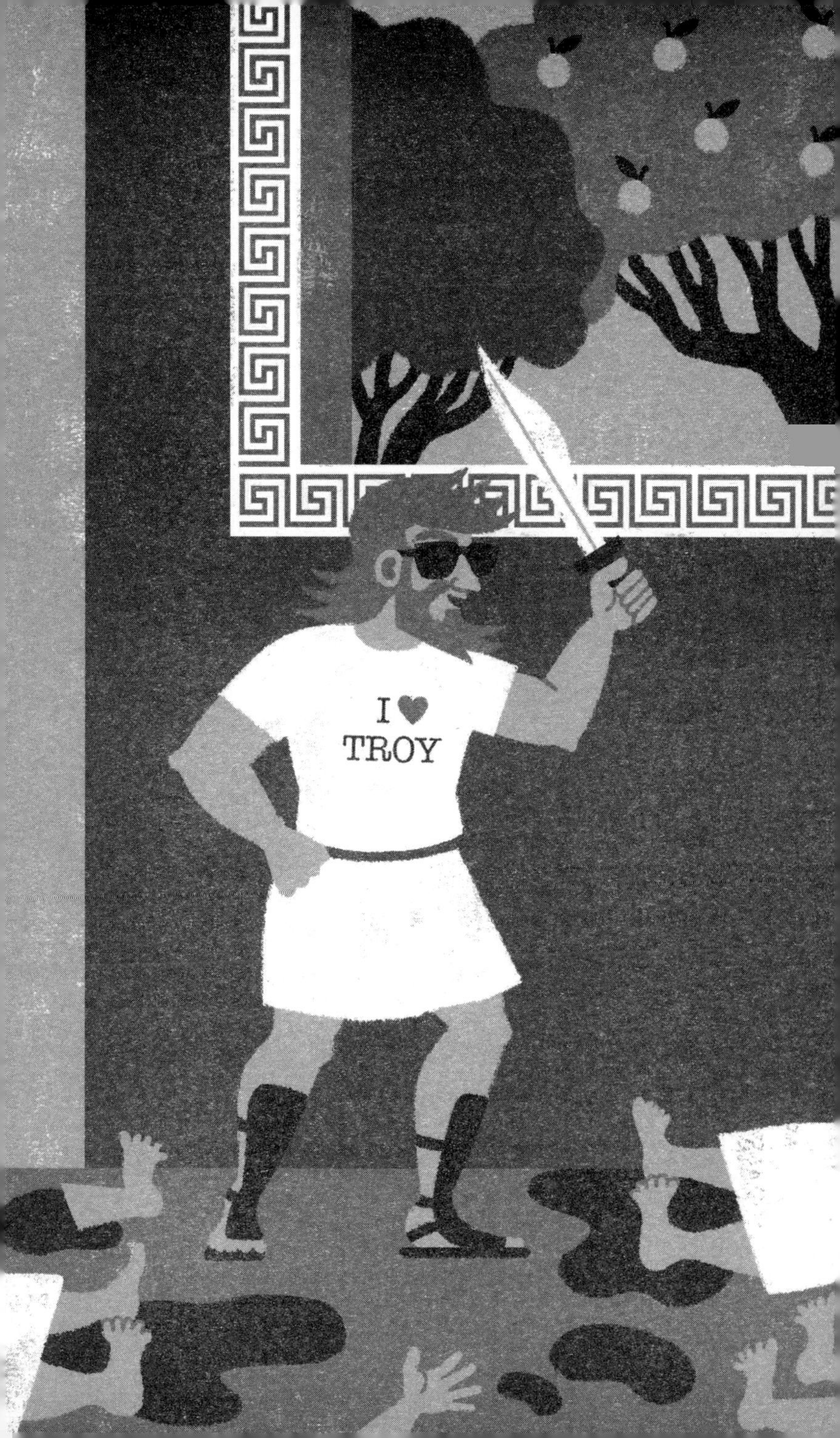
I ♥
TROY

ODYSSEUS AND PENELOPE REUNITE

'So, honeybun,' Odysseus asks, 'what have *you* done for the last twenty years? Jeez, you haven't even finished that weaving.'

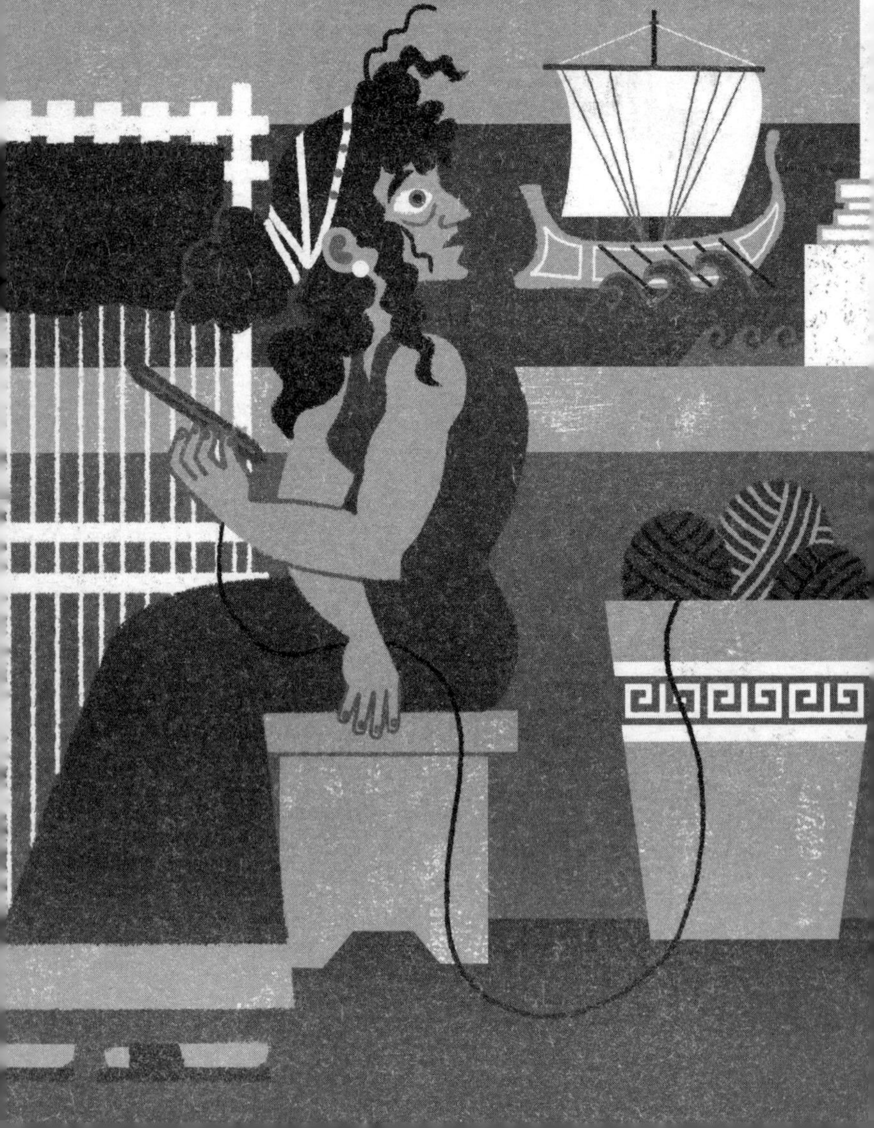

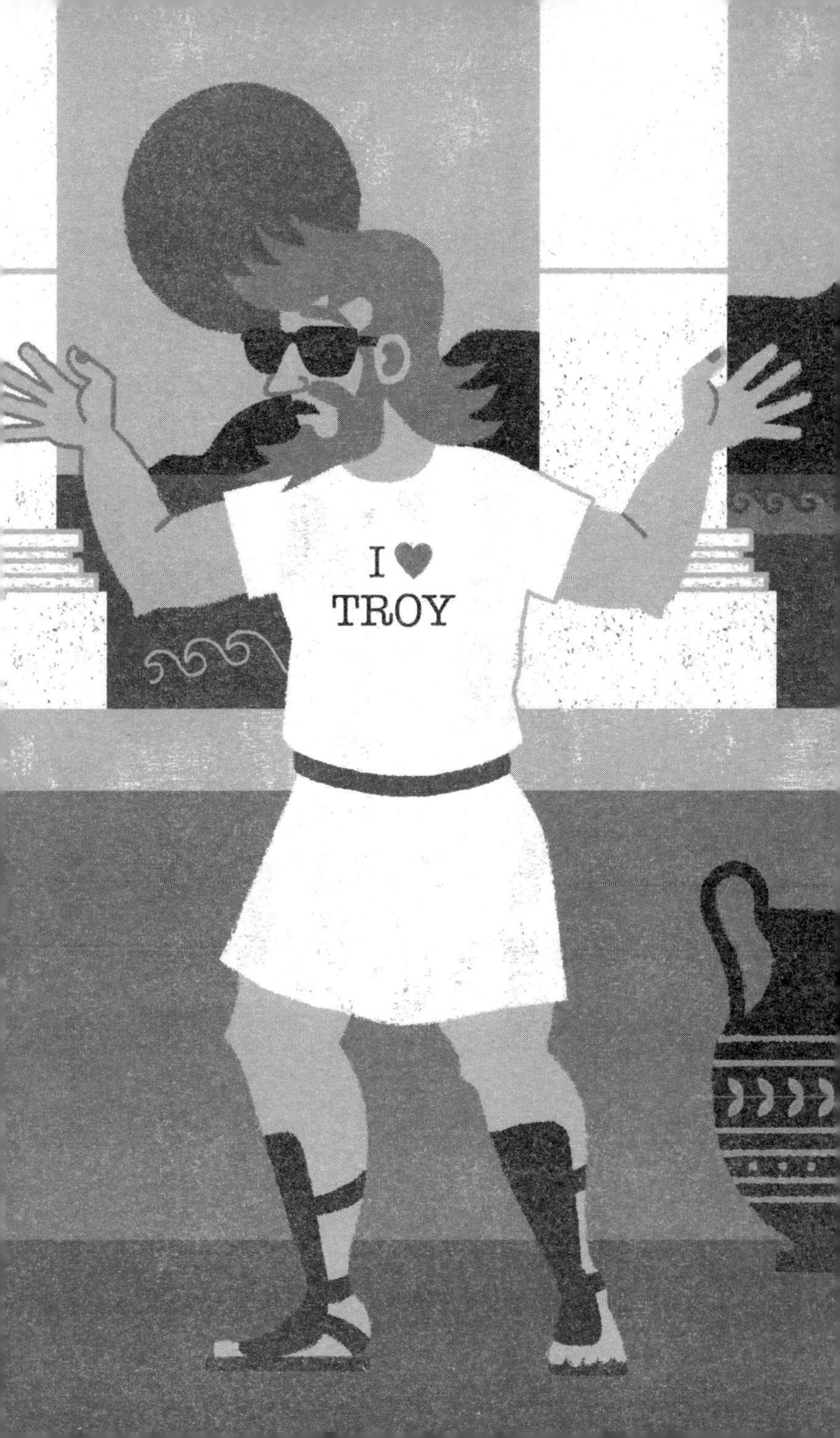
I ♥
TROY

The end.